STAR WARS®

SMUGGLER'S RUN

A HAN SOLO & CHEWBACCA ADVENTURE

WRITTEN BY **GREG RUCKA**   ILLUSTRATED BY **PHIL NOTO**

First published in Great Britain 2015
by Egmont UK Limited, The Yellow Building,
1 Nicholas Road, London W11 4AN

© and ™ 2015 Lucasfilm Ltd.

ISBN 978 1 4052 7785 3
60549/1
Printed in Italy

Cover design by Richie Hull
Designed by Jason Wojtowicz

To find more great *Star Wars* books, visit www.egmont.co.uk/starwars

Stay safe online. Any website addresses listed in this book are correct at the time of going to print. However, Egmont is not responsible for content hosted by third parties. Please be aware that online content can be subject to change and websites can contain content that is unsuitable for children. We advise that all children are supervised when using the internet.

A long time ago in a galaxy far, far away. . . .

It is a period of civil war. The heroic
freedom fighters of the REBEL ALLIANCE
have won their most important victory thus far
with the destruction of the Empire's ultimate weapon,
the DEATH STAR.

But the Rebellion has no time to savor its victory.
The evil Galactic Empire has recognized the threat
the rebels pose, and is now searching the galaxy
for any and all information that will lead
to the final destruction of the freedom fighters.

For the *MILLENNIUM FALCON*'s crew,
who saved the life of Luke Skywalker
during the Battle of Yavin,
their involvement with the rebels is at an end.
Now HAN SOLO and CHEWBACCA hope
to take their reward and settle some old debts. . . .

PROLOGUE

T HE OLD MAN at the cantina had many years of practice keeping his head down and his ears open, and he'd been doing both for a couple of hours now.

The bar was called Serendipity, and the conversations taking place around him were quiet, respectful of the space and the other patrons both. He could catch bits and pieces, odd words that reached him, spoken in any smattering of the galaxy's languages. Some of them he knew well, others not at all. There was an Ithorian who had come in shortly after he had, now sitting at a table with a Dug and speaking animatedly, his voice a low bass rumble the old man could feel in his chest; a Bith, a Neimoidian, and an Advosze, all apparently talking business they didn't want overheard; a Twi'lek male whispering sweet nothings in a Devaronian's ear.

And three humans, two male and one female, who'd arrived in the past half hour like they owned the place, were now seated maybe two meters from the old man's back. They were already on their third round and getting loud. From his stool at the bar, he could see them clearly reflected in the mirror behind the bartender's shelves of liquors rare and common.

"Speed," one of the men said. This was the burly one, maybe early forties in standard years. He was dressed like the other two, in a combination of mismatched Imperial uniforms, bits of salvaged armor, and a heavy blast vest. They all wore blast vests—same colors, same insignia.

Mercenaries, the old man thought, or perhaps a gang, swoop or otherwise.

"That's what it all comes down to," the burly one continued. "Speed, nothing more."

"Garbage." This was the woman, youngest of the group and, by the looks of her, the meanest, too. All three were armed, but she had the shaft of a vibro-axe strapped to her back in addition to the heavy blaster holstered along the left side of her torso. She was blond, and perhaps because of that she reminded the old man at the bar of someone he'd dealt with years before. Not the same woman, of course—this one was far too young—but the memory came back all the same, as if it were yesterday.

"You remember Rigger?" the woman said. "You remember what happened to him? You remember the *Streak*?"

"I remember," said the other male, who was somewhere between the ages of the burly one and the woman. He was big and broad shouldered, and his scalp was shaved to reveal a tattoo of a Twi'lek female sprawled on her belly, her face near his forehead, blowing a kiss. To the old man watching the three reflected in the mirror, it looked like the tattoo was flirting with him.

"So not speed," the woman said.

"*Streak* was fast," said the burly one.

"Sure, it was fast." The man with the tattoo said, finishing his drink. "It slammed right into the side of that canyon going like it was fire."

"Don't mean nothing if it won't maneuver," the woman said. "You want a ship like the *Nebula Wisp*, or maybe . . . what was its name? You know the one I'm talking about?"

The burly one said, "The *Black Box*?"

"No, no. . . ." The woman trailed off, picking at a fingernail that, even from that distance, the old man could see was filth-encrusted. She brightened suddenly. "The *Fourth Pass*! That's the one! They say she'd stop on a credit and give you change."

The tattooed one grunted and looked into his empty

glass. At the bar, the old man caught the bartender's eye, then indicated his own drink with a finger, asking for a refill. The bartender grinned.

"Defense," the tattooed one said. "You can be fast, you can be maneuverable, but sooner or later, you're gonna get hit. You can't take the hit, that's it—show's over."

"They can't hit what they can't catch," the woman said.

"They'll hit it eventually," the tattooed man persisted. "You got enough guns pointing at you, you're gonna be nothing but scrap floating in a vacuum. Doesn't matter how fast you are, doesn't matter if you twist and turn. Eventually, you're gonna get hit."

"That's what we need," the burly one said. "We need a ship that can do all three. We need a triple threat."

The woman laughed. "Good luck. Doesn't exist."

"Sure it does." The burly one leaned forward. "You know it does. I know it does. Even Strater knows it does."

The tattooed one—presumably Strater—shook his empty glass, as if hoping that would magically refill it, then nodded.

"The *Millennium Falcon*," Strater said.

"The *Millennium Falcon*," the others agreed.

The old man sighed loudly—loudly enough to grab all three humans' attention. He heard chairs scrape as they turned to look at him. The bartender set a refill in front of the old man and took his almost-empty glass away.

"You got something you want to add, grandpa?" the woman asked.

The old man sipped his drink. "You'll never catch her."

The tattooed one, Strater, leaned back in his chair. "Think we've got a better chance of that than you, old man."

"And even if you did catch her, you'd never be able to fly her," the old man said, as if he hadn't heard.

"If it's got engines, we can fly it." The woman was getting annoyed; he could see it in her face, reflected over the bartender's shoulder.

The bartender gave the old man a warning look that clearly said she did not want to have to clean up a mess.

"A ship is more than engines, more than shields or armor or maneuver jets or its hyperdrive or anything else." The old man picked up his drink, ignoring the bartender, then turned and stood. "A ship is all those things, but it's nothing if it doesn't have the right crew."

"I told you, we can fly it." The woman was looking him over suspiciously. Again, the old man found himself thinking of someone else from long ago—someone with one eye that had viewed everything suspiciously.

The old man pulled out the empty chair and sat down between Strater and the woman, facing the burly one. He grinned, rubbed the scar on his chin with one hand, then raised his glass in the other and drained it.

"Nah," the old man said.

"And you're so certain?" the burly one asked.

"Pretty certain, yeah."

"How's that?"

The old man tilted his chair onto its back legs and looked around the bar. No one else was listening. No one else was paying attention. At the door, the bouncer had turned away and was watching the entrance while scratching behind one ear with a paw. The old man turned the empty glass in his hand, as if considering its potential, or at least lamenting its emptiness.

"You buy me a drink," the old man said, "and I'll tell you a story about the *Millennium Falcon*."

They bought him a drink and listened.

PART
ONE

CHAPTER 01
WAITING TO HURRY

THE WOOKIEE SIGHED, a low rumble, and gazed at the medal in his palm. On the humans it looked substantial and solid, fit to be worn around the neck. In his hand the scale was altered, and if he brought his fingers together he could conceal it entirely. A pretty thing, hastily engraved in a stylized flower meant perhaps to recall the emblem of the Republic. At its heart a rising sun, halfway above the horizon, both symbolized the dawn of a new hope in the wake of this victory over the Galactic Empire and recalled the Death Star's destruction.

He sighed a second time, tucked the award into the satchel that hung from the bandolier of bowcaster ammunition slung over his left shoulder, and leaned forward in his seat to peer out the cockpit of the *Millennium Falcon*. Outside, rebels ran back and forth across the hangar, hastily preparing their evacuation. The base on Yavin 4 was, to put it mildly, compromised. With the destruction of the Death Star, it would be a day at most—perhaps even less—before the Imperial fleet arrived to reduce anything they found to rubble and dust. While they might still have been flushed with their victory, the Rebellion's high command knew better than to believe they could repel, or even withstand, such an assault. They had been lucky with the Death Star, and it had cost them all the same. They wouldn't get lucky twice. The plan, as the Wookiee understood it, was for the band of freedom fighters to scatter across the galaxy in as many directions as they could manage at once, with the goal of meeting up again at a later date, and preferably in a much safer place.

He huffed to himself, wondering how the rebels hoped to survive. Their own fleet—and he used the word generously—was already scattered. All that remained on the fourth moon of Yavin were the three snub fighters—two X-wings and a single Y-wing—that had made it through the battle, plus some three dozen or so transports of various shapes, makes, and sizes, all of which had been past their prime even before the fall of the Republic.

The Wookiee didn't fancy their chances.

That said, he understood their fire. He was a Wookiee, after all, and he knew passion. His were a proud people, a people who had lived for hundreds of years peacefully on their wooded homeworld of Kashyyyk until the Clone Wars. He had been younger then, just one hundred and eighty, and he had fought the Separatist battle droids. He had witnessed the betrayal of the clones and the beginning of the Empire. He had seen his people, his brothers and sisters, his family, put in chains and sold as slaves throughout the galaxy. He had been put in chains himself, and just the memory of it made a growl rise in his throat.

So he understood the Rebellion. In truth, he would be standing with them if it weren't for two things: the Corellian and the ship. He wouldn't abandon either of them. He was bound to both, as they were to him.

Han Solo had not been a man to inspire trust when they'd first met. He'd been a fast-talker, smug, even arrogant. He had seemed more interested in looking out for himself than in looking out for others. "Enlightened self-interest" was how Solo himself had described it.

"I don't take an interest in my own well-being in this galaxy, nobody else is gonna do it for me, pal," he had said.

Even with that, though, Solo had proven the Wookiee wrong. He'd proven him wrong when the two of them had fled to the Outer Rim to survive amidst bounty hunters, pirates, and fellow smugglers, trying to scratch out a living wage working for the Hutts. He'd proven him wrong time and again, and if the Wookiee had learned one thing about his friend and partner, it was that there was no telling what the Corellian would care about, or why. Despite all his posturing and swagger, there was a core to Han Solo as golden as the medals they'd all received for their part in the recent battle.

The comm on the control console overhead lit up, flashing blue and bleating its odd singsong. On other ships, the comm would just chirp incessantly, calling for attention, but the *Falcon* was not, and never had been, like other ships. Just another of her idiosyncrasies, another of the things that made him love her so.

That was the second reason, of course: this ship.

When the boy from Tatooine, Skywalker, had seen the *Falcon* for the first time back in Mos Eisley, he'd described it as "a piece of junk." Solo had taken it personally, but the Wookiee could understand why Luke had thought so. He didn't agree, of course, but he understood. The *Falcon* looked like just another Corellian YT-1300 light freighter, and there had to be thousands, if not hundreds of thousands, of them in service throughout the galaxy. Her cockpit, for reasons no one but the designers back at Corell Industries could understand, was posted to the starboard side, and jutted at an odd angle instead of being mounted on the center line. Her engines were overpowered for her size, but her controls were so sensitive as to be paranoid, which meant she was temperamental and needed a pilot *and* copilot to manage her in flight. Even then she was liable to slip out of control if both operators didn't know exactly what they were doing.

That was just the YT-1300 series as a whole.

But the *Falcon* took all those characteristics and multiplied them exponentially. She was bruised. She was dented. She needed paint and near-constant maintenance. Easily half the money they pulled in doing runs for Jabba the Hutt or whoever else went to upkeep, new parts, fuel. She drank fuel like she'd been wandering the Dune Sea for weeks without water. Her gravity emulators had an annoying—and, frankly, alarming—tendency to cut out during sharp maneuvering, which would send you across the cabin if you weren't strapped in when it happened. The multiple computers that worked to keep everything on the ship running in concert not only had developed, over the years, their own dialects, but at times seemed to feud among themselves. And you didn't want to get the Wookiee started on the state of the ion flux stabilizers, or the way the Duvo-Pek acceleration compensators would not just seek to compensate but would instead do precisely the *opposite*.

Oh, but she was *fast*.

She was the fastest ship he'd ever flown—had ever

seen. She cut through space and atmosphere alike as if born to it, and seated side by side, he and Solo could make her dance in ways that would've made those designers back in the day on Corellia drop their jaws. They had modified almost every single part of the engines—from the bolts to the main drive—coaxing, teasing more power, more speed. They had taken her apart and put her back together more times than the Wookiee could count, and each time the *Falcon* had rewarded them by giving more in return, by urging them to push her further.

He loved this ship.

Reaching with one long arm, the Wookiee slapped the flashing comm button and snarled a greeting, asking Solo what was taking him so long.

"Oh my! Chewbacca, wherever did you learn such language?"

The Wookiee chuckled. It wasn't Solo calling, but the protocol droid.

"Captain Solo asks you to join him in the briefing room."

The Wookiee frowned and growled his response.

"I'm sure I don't have the first idea," C-3PO answered. "He says that you need to join him at once, because the princess won't take no for an answer and he feels it would be more persuasive coming from you."

The Wookiee grinned, mostly because he knew there was nobody to see it. Those two had been at each other from the moment they'd met. This explained things. They were supposed to have lifted off more than an hour earlier to make their way back to Tatooine. Between the reward money for rescuing the princess from the Death Star and the fee they'd been promised for the Alderaan run besides, they had more than enough money to square things with Jabba. Enough, even, to get back into his good graces and have him call off the bounty hunters he had already set on their trail. But that would work only if they brought the money *to* Jabba; if the bounty hunters brought them in first, it would be a different situation entirely.

Jabba didn't deal kindly with those who owed him money. He'd take their freedom and maybe their lives, and he'd definitely take the *Falcon*. None of those outcomes appealed to the Wookiee. He knew for a fact that they appealed to Solo even less.

The Wookiee barked a response to C-3PO, slapped the comm button again, and swung up from his seat, ducking out of habit as he stepped out of the cockpit and knocked the pair of novelty chance dice that he'd hung there as a joke some years ago. There was only one thing that would make Han Solo delay their departure, and that was a pretty girl.

He had to admit, he was curious to find out just what the pretty girl wanted.

"I'm not part of this!" Han Solo said. "I'm not a part of your rebellion, I'm not a freedom fighter, and I don't work for you, Your Highness!"

Princess Leia Organa of Alderaan took two quick steps forward, her face tilting up to glare at the smuggler. If Solo's nearly half a meter of height over her impressed her at all, it didn't show. She raised an index finger, directing it at the smuggler as if contemplating poking him in the eye.

"If you worked for me," she said, "I'd have fired you already."

"If I worked for you, lady, I'd have quit." Solo crossed his arms, certain he had, for the moment, claimed the last word.

The princess remained motionless for a moment, using a glare that had once, he imagined, reduced her opponents in the now-dissolved Imperial Senate to tears. One of the rebel soldiers busy dismantling the control room edged past, her arms full of equipment, carefully avoiding eye contact. During the battle, the room had been cluttered with displays tracking the Death Star's relentless approach to the Yavin moon, monitors broadcasting the pilot chatter as fighter after fighter had been lost, downed by anti-starship fire or the precision work of their TIE opponents. The base, as Solo understood it, had been set up in a temple to the gods of the long-forgotten and long-dead people of Yavin 4. The rebels had found it and made it the heart of their operations. Now it would again be what it was, a legacy to those lost and forgotten.

A battered service droid whined its way past carrying one of the monitors, and Leia took that as an excuse to break their staring contest, turning away in barely disguised disgust. She was angry and not afraid to show it, and Solo had to admit he took a certain pleasure in winding her up. Her buttons were so easy to press. She was, undoubtedly, one of the most beautiful women he had ever met, and coming from Han Solo that actually meant something, because he'd seen a lot of the galaxy and his share of beautiful women. That she was smart, brave—perhaps, given her position in the Rebellion, suicidally so—and gave as good as she got only made her more attractive to him. She was also as stubborn as a gundark, and he appreciated that, too. In fact, he kinda liked her, especially with all they had recently been through together with the kid and the old man.

But there was absolutely no way he was going to tell *her* that, especially when she was trying to guilt him into maybe dying for a cause he had no part in and wanted no part of.

One of the doors into the makeshift, and now diminishing, control room opened, and a trio of soldiers carted more equipment out as Chewbacca ducked his head to step inside. Solo caught his partner's eye, and the Wookiee nodded slightly in greeting.

Princess Leia watched the Wookiee's approach, tracking him to Solo's side, then turned fully to face the smuggler again.

"People will die." She said it simply, a statement of truth, looking at him with those brown eyes that seemed to see everything.

"I don't know them," Solo said.

For an instant—just an instant—he saw the disappointment on her face and felt something dangerously close to guilt.

"Let me ask you something," Leia said to the Wookiee. She jerked a thumb in Solo's direction. "Is there actually a heart beating in there, or just a safe where he keeps his credits?"

Chewbacca snorted, then looked to Solo, canting his head. He barked.

"Oh, no, no," Solo said. "You haven't heard what it is she wants us to do, Chewie. Go ahead, Your Shining Royalness, tell him about this little suicide mission you've got up your sleeve."

"It's not a suicide mission, not if you follow the plan." Leia tapped the control on the main battle display, one of the only pieces of equipment still remaining and powered, and only because it would take the help of another half dozen droids to move it. The display illuminated, showing a map of the galaxy. She tapped the console again, this time working quickly, and together Solo and Chewbacca watched as the map zoomed down, rescaling itself over and over again, to center on a section of the Outer Rim. With a final press of a button the map froze, displaying a system of six planets.

"Cyrkon, in the Outer Rim, on the edge of Hutt Space," Leia said, indicating the second planet from the system's star. "Outside the Imperial sphere, so it gets a lot of traffic from people like you."

Chewbacca snuffed.

"She means smugglers," Solo said.

"No, I mean criminals," Leia said.

Chewbacca raised an eyebrow.

"The problem with being a rebellion is that we don't have resources," Leia said, staring at the projection. "And what we do have is never enough. We have to stay on the move. We're dealing with it now, with this evacuation—you see it all around you. The Empire has *everything*, all of the resources, all of the troops, all of the spies. For us to survive, we have to plan not just one move or three moves but five moves ahead. We have to have contingencies. Not just where we're going next, but where we *might* be going if that location is compromised, if it falls through. We have to have options."

"If you're planning on hiding your rebellion on Cyrkon, it's going to be a short one," Solo said. "Too close to the Hutts—they'll sell you out in a second."

She looked from the map long enough to shoot Solo another withering glare. "Thank you, Captain, for that brilliant strategic insight." She motioned to the map. "Cyrkon isn't the location of the next rebel base."

"You're smarter than you act."

She ignored him, tapping the controls again. The map shifted to the side, and a new image sprang into place. A holo of a human male, roughly twenty standard years old. Solo didn't recognize him.

"This is Lieutenant Ematt, leader of the Shrikes." Leia paused, staring at the holo. "The Shrikes are special recon for the Rebellion. It's a small team, and their mission is very simple. They're responsible for identifying, securing, and preparing new locations for the Rebellion. They compile the list. They pick the rendezvous points. They explore all the options."

"That's a lot of very sensitive information for one man to be carrying," Solo said.

"Yes. It's also one of the only ways for us to remain secure. The fewer people who know a secret, the fewer who can give it away."

Chewie rumbled agreement.

"But he knows, Han, do you understand? Ematt knows not only where we're going, but where we *might* be going. He knows the rendezvous points. He knows where we've hidden weapons, food, medicine. He knows all of it."

Solo nodded. Something was turning sour in his stomach, as if he'd eaten a meal he maybe shouldn't have. He had a bad feeling about this.

"The Shrikes were ambushed by the Imperial Security Bureau on Taanab," the princess said. "Ematt escaped the ambush, but the rest of his team were killed. He managed to get a burst transmission to us, letting us know what happened, letting us know that he's made it off-planet, on his way to Cyrkon. But the ISB is on his trail, he's alone, and he's exposed."

Chewie huffed softly, under his voice. He and Solo both could see this coming.

"The *Falcon* is the only ship fast enough to reach Cyrkon in time." She pressed the controls on the map once more and the images winked out. She turned to look at them—first Chewie, then Han. "If the ISB captures Ematt, they'll get everything. They'll torture him. They'll drug him. They'll get everything. It will be the end of the Rebellion."

She wasn't angry anymore. She wasn't pleading, she wasn't begging. She was just looking at them, at Solo and his friend and partner, waiting. She'd made her argument.

Solo preferred it when she was angry.

Chewbacca growled, a short string of barks that ended in a heavy rumble.

Solo looked at him in amazement. "Think this one through, Chewie."

The Wookiee snuffed.

Solo shook his head. "You're supposed to back me up, not side with her!"

The Wookiee snuffed again.

Solo couldn't believe this. "She's asking us to fly into a system on the edge of Hutt Space to rescue a guy who maybe is already dead, never mind that the ISB is after him! Never mind that Cyrkon is teeming with the worst scum this galaxy has to offer. Never mind that Jabba's got bounty hunters taking numbers to come after us, if he hasn't sent them already—"

Chewbacca grunted and barked.

"I know it's the Outer Rim! I know it's on the way, but even if we succeed we'll have to take him to the rendezvous point, or else it's not much of a rescue! This isn't our fight, pal!"

This time the Wookiee remained silent, just looking at Solo with those blue eyes.

Leia was looking at him, too.

Solo sighed. *Some fights*, he thought, *you just can't win*.

"We're going to need the pass phrase, whatever it is, so Ematt will recognize us," Solo said. He tried not to sound petulant.

Leia smiled as if she'd known all along he'd say yes. Solo scowled.

"And I expect to be paid for this," he added.

CHAPTER 02
THE PRIDE OF THE ISB

COMMANDER ALECIA BECK was, as far as she was concerned, a very good officer for the Imperial Security Bureau. She didn't have a choice. Never mind that she was a woman—and there were very few of those holding high ranks in the Empire—hers was a job that did not tolerate failure. For the Empire to work, loyalty had to be ensured. For the Empire to thrive, everyone had to do their part. For the Empire to endure, its enemies had to be hunted down and destroyed.

Relentlessly.

She was glad to do this. She took pride in doing this, the same way she took pride in the perfect condition of her jet-black uniform and the gleam of the rank insignia on her left breast. She even took pride in the scar that ran in an almost straight line from just below her hairline—blond hair in a perfect regulation cut, of course—and down her left cheek. The same way she took pride in the artificial eye that had replaced her ruined left one. It was proof of her loyalty, and her commitment, and she knew the agents and stormtroopers who served under her command told the story to every new recruit who came aboard. How Commander Beck, during her first tour with the ISB, had caught her training officer selling secrets for credits. How she had confronted him, he a full captain and she only a lieutenant, in the maintenance bay aboard the *Vehement*. How he had tried to kill her with a laser cutter from the nearby workbench.

How they had fought. How she had won.

She'd received a promotion and a commendation for that.

So, yes, she was proud.

"Search the bodies," Beck ordered.

The stormtrooper sergeant at her side, designation TX-828, came to rigid attention. "Yes, ma'am."

She watched him peel off, directing the eight members of the troop as she had ordered. They moved briskly, efficiently, precisely as they had been trained. She turned her attention to the body at her feet, a female Rodian lying in a pool of her own green blood. Beck shifted the vision in her cybernetic eye and let it scroll through different spectrums, infrared showing heat leaving the corpse. The woman was dressed as a commoner: low-class, filthy clothes. Beck pushed the body with her foot, rolling the woman onto her back. One of her arms flopped to the side. Suction-tipped fingers released the long-barreled sporting blaster the Rodian had held as she died.

Beck flicked her vision to ultraviolet, her eye making a soft, audible click, then lowered herself to one knee and took hold of the woman's wrist. She made a face as she did this. She didn't like most aliens, but this Rodian, in particular, made her angry even in death. She yanked back the woman's cuff, exposing her forearm. There, visible in the UV spectrum, was the marking Beck hoped she would find—the spread wings of a bird of prey—a shrike. She released her hold and returned to her feet, frowning to herself.

She had been correct, then.

She looked at the ship the rebels had been trying to escape in, a small, ugly transport that looked barely capable of reaching hyperspace, let alone staying there.

"Sergeant, with me," Beck said.

"Ma'am."

They made their way aboard.

Part of the pleasure Beck took in her job was that it let her be smart. There were parts of the Imperial Army and Imperial Navy where being smart was a liability.

Seeing too much, hearing too much, or asking the wrong questions could get you into a lot of trouble. In the ISB the rules were much the same, in truth, but with a difference: you could be smart, if you were smart at your job. Beck, who as a child had wanted to be a detective, found this part of the work especially enjoyable. Rooting out traitors to the Empire was just solving another kind of mystery.

She forced herself to go slowly through the transport, moving from the cockpit to the cargo hold, checking each of the small berths as she went, even though she knew time was of the essence. Whatever had happened in the Yavin system she didn't know, but the rumors were flying, and that morning's communiqué from Coruscant had been very clear to all ISB commands.

BY ORDER OF THE EMPEROR
To: All Imperial Security Bureau Senior Commanders
PRIORITY ONE
The Emperor commands that all known and suspected terrorists or terrorist sympathizers affiliated with the self-named Rebel Alliance be immediately arrested and detained for interrogation on the charge of treason.

This directive supersedes any ongoing operations.
EFFECTIVE IMMEDIATELY

This meant, whatever had happened in the Yavin system, it had been bad for the Empire. It also meant that Beck's very careful tracking of this particular rebel cell was at an end. She had hoped to keep them under surveillance until they could lead her back to even bigger fish, perhaps even the Rebellion's high command itself, but the directive had been unequivocal: she was to move on them, and to move on them now.

Beck thought once more of the Rodian woman, dead in the bay outside of the ship, and felt herself growing angry again. When Beck and her squad had arrived in the hangar bay here on Taanab they'd found the transport in preflight preparations, four of the crew of rebels disconnecting the fuel lines and loading equipment. She hadn't gotten as far as shouting, "Stop, you're all under arrest!" before the shooting had started. If the rebels had had an ounce of sense, they would've surrendered, but no, they had to fight, and despite the stormtroopers' setting their E-11 blaster rifles to stun, not one rebel had been taken alive.

It had been a furious, if brief, firefight—over in less than ten seconds—with not one of Beck's men wounded and the four rebels laid out on the ground, stunned. Beck had ordered the sergeant to put the binders to them when, from the roof of the transport, she'd spotted motion and drawn her blaster. There had been the Rodian atop the ship. Before Beck or any of the stormtroopers could react, the alien had opened fire. But she hadn't shot at them.

She had shot each of Beck's prisoners.

One after the other, the Rodian had put a blaster bolt into men and women who must've been her friends, her comrades-in-arms. Before the stormtroopers could bring their rifles up, it was already over. In an instant, Beck had gone from four prisoners to no prisoners.

"Stop!" Beck had shouted.

The Rodian had looked at Beck with those enormous eyes, then put her blaster to her own temple.

Beck could do nothing but watch her fall.

She should have had five prisoners for interrogation. Instead she had none.

Whatever they knew, the Rodian had been willing both to kill and die to protect it. Beck was certain it was important. So she took her time walking through the transport, taking in the details, and when she'd done it once, she did it a second time. The bodies had been removed from the bay by the time she exited the ship, and the sergeant immediately came to attention at her side.

"There's one missing," Beck said.

"All the rebels are accounted for, ma'am."

Beck didn't bother to correct him. She knew what she knew. The transport was an EE-730, made by Kuat, equipped to berth six passengers and crew total.

All six beds had shown signs of occupants. Five bodies had been taken away. One, therefore, was missing.

"Land ten more squads from *Vehement* immediately. I want a sweep of all the landing bays, all the local cantinas, the normal drill. No ships are to take off or land until I give the word."

"Yes, ma'am."

"And send a scanning crew aboard with a data retrieval team immediately. I want everything from the computers, especially from the navicomputer, as well as the hyperspace logs. Have them sent to my office aboard *Vehement*."

"Yes, ma'am."

She headed out of the bay but stopped before she'd taken two steps, her eyes falling to the pool of drying blood, what remained to mark the Rodian's death. Some people, Beck thought, would've thought the Rodian brave. Some people might even have used words like *self-sacrifice* and *noble* to describe what the alien had done. Beck thought those people were idiots, perhaps even traitors. She smeared the toe of her boot in the blood, feeling that anger again.

"Fool," she said.

"We are not a blockade ship," Captain Hove said. "We are not equipped to interdict flights to and from Taanab."

"Find a way," Beck said.

"I take this to mean the operation was not as successful as you might've hoped?"

"There was an unexpected complication." Beck moved past him, into her office aboard the *Vehement*, and settled behind her desk. At her back, the wide porthole showed a view of Taanab turning beneath them, framed by a limitless field of stars stretching out toward infinity beyond. She turned her seat to admire the view, but further to avoid Hove's gaze. While the Star Destroyer *Vehement* was technically his command, falling under the umbrella of the Imperial Navy, there was no doubt as to which of them was truly in charge. For that reason, among others—chief of them being Hove's terror at doing anything Beck might feel the need to report to the ISB high command as suspicious or even treasonous—he did not like her, and their relationship was defined by a cordial, and cool, formality.

"Admiral Ozzel has issued a communiqué to the fleet ordering us to battle readiness," Hove said. "If you have information that you aren't sharing with me, I'd ask, for the good of this vessel, that you reconsider."

Beck arched an eyebrow. Outside, a two-ship element of TIE fighters swooped past, flying sentry in perfect parallel formation.

"You'll know what you need to know when you need

to know it, Captain." Beck swiveled back around to face Hove. "Burdening you with too much information is an invitation to leak that information to the enemies of the Empire. And you wouldn't want that."

Hove stiffened, and Beck managed to keep herself from smiling.

"No, Commander," he said.

"I require an astromech droid sent to me immediately, and I require you on the bridge. When I give the order, I expect us to move out at once."

"The ship, as ever, is at your disposal."

"Yes," Beck said. "It is. An astromech, now."

He snapped his heels together, pivoted, and exited the office, the doors sliding emphatically shut in his wake. Beck turned her attention to her computer, which displayed the reports sent up from the surface and the data recovered from the transport. Once she had reviewed the information she used her comm to contact the squad sergeant.

"TX-828," he answered.

"Sergeant, I've just reviewed the transport's records. Is this everything?"

"Yes, ma'am."

"No, it isn't. It's missing the logs from the navi-computer."

"No, ma'am."

"The log is empty, Sergeant."

"Yes, ma'am, that is correct. Best the data retrieval team could determine, there'd been a hard wipe on the system within the last day. They say there are signs that the navicomputer had its cache wiped regularly."

Her door beeped, and Beck spared a glance toward the surveillance monitor, showing her the view outside her office. An R4 model astromech droid, shiny black and silver, waited outside. She keyed the lock, letting the droid inside.

"And the same goes for the hyperspace logs, I presume?"

"That's correct, ma'am."

She killed the connection and pointed at the R4 unit.

"Plug into my local, access all the data that's just been uploaded from the operation on the surface," Beck said.

The droid whistled and rolled closer, its top swiveling as its computer interface arm extended from its body to plug into the port at the side of her desk. The unit released a longer stream of binary chirps and whistles, and Beck went back to looking out her window, thinking. Wiping the navicomputer wasn't unheard of, but hard wiping took time and was done only to prevent exactly what Beck was trying to accomplish: retrieval of the ship's history. More than that, the library files could be corrupted by such a wipe, and that, in turn, could lead to a disastrous hyperspace jump. Disastrous hyperspace jumps normally ended with the ship's crew dead and the ship in fragments.

The rebels had worked very, very hard to hide their trail. The Rodian had been willing to kill and die to keep their secrets. All of this and the tattoo of the shrike, visible only to those who would know to look for it. It could only mean one thing.

"Ematt," Beck said. "You were there. Where did you go?"

As if in answer the R4 unit emitted what, to Beck, sounded like a triumphant string of beeps, drawing her attention back to her desk and the monitor there. Despite its best efforts, the droid had failed to recover any data from the navicomputer or the hyperspace logs; instead, it had taken the data from the ship's supplies and stores, in particular the fuel store, and cross-referenced that with the EE-730's flight range.

"That tells me where they've been," Beck told the droid. "Not where they were heading. Not where he's gone. Link to the bridge computer on my authority. I want a list of all vessels that left the planet between the time we assaulted the transport and the time I ordered the blockade in place."

The droid whined.

Beck considered. The rebels had been preparing to leave Taanab when she and the stormtroopers had arrived. Ematt must've fled the ship the moment the attack started. The stormtroopers on the surface had reported nothing, and she could only guess how many ships Captain Hove had let leave the planet before she'd ordered the blockade in place.

He was off-world by now—she knew it.

The droid chirped and swiveled its head, using the projector to display three stacked images: three ships that had left the planet in the gap before Hove had begun the blockade. One was an automated droid transport, on a fixed run toward the Inner Rim, and Beck dismissed that one right away; it would be beyond foolish for Ematt to flee *toward* the heart of Imperial control. Of the remaining two, one was an old Sienar MK I bulk transport. The second was a Kuat Yards hauler, a pure cargo ferry, designed to move hundreds of units of freight in their own separate containers.

It would be very easy to hide inside one of those containers until the hauler reached its destination.

"That one," Beck pointed. "Plot its jump and all destinations along the route."

The droid had apparently been anticipating this, and immediately the ships vanished, replaced by a star map with the hauler's projected flight path. Farther out toward the Outer Rim, on a line to Hutt Space.

Beck sat back. She would track the Sienar's flight path as well, just to be thorough, but she was already certain. She keyed the comm on her desk. "Captain?"

"Yes, Commander?"

"Set course for Cyrkon," she said. "I want to be there yesterday."

CHAPTER 03
WHAT COULD POSSIBLY
GO WRONG?

HAN SOLO SCOWLED and stared out the cockpit of the *Millennium Falcon* at the swirling blue-and-white hyperspace tunnel, not really seeing it. He could feel the ship around him, the low vibration of the heavily modified Isu-Sim engines growling, hurtling them faster than lightspeed. He thought about the old man, and what he'd been trying to teach the kid on their way from Tatooine to Alderaan—the trip that had started this whole mess, as far as Solo was concerned. The old man had talked of the Force, telling the kid that he needed to stretch out with his senses, garbage like that. Solo didn't need the Force to feel what the *Falcon* was doing. It was in his bones.

Chewie rumbled at him, trying for the third time to engage him conversation.

"I'm not talking to you," Solo said.

The Wookiee chuffed.

"I'm not sulking," Solo snapped. Even to his own ears, it sounded sullen.

The Wookiee laughed.

"We'll see how funny you think this is when we're rotting in some Imperial detention cell. This was never the plan, pal."

The engines shifted subtly, almost imperceptibly, but both of them felt it, and both of them straightened up in their seats, Chewbacca already reaching overhead to lock in the acceleration compensators as Solo reached forward to throttle back out of hyperspace. There was no need to talk; they'd done this a thousand times. You could tell the quality of a crew by how they handled this maneuver. There were pilots who earned very comfortable livings flying rich passengers here and there solely on the basis of how smoothly they could switch from hyperspace back to realspace, without spilling their passengers' drinks. Only the very best could manage it seamlessly.

Solo eased the throttle handles back, cutting power on each engine in concert and watching as the end of the hyperspace tunnel suddenly ran toward them, a field of stars and the glow of the atmosphere of Cyrkon coming into focus. At the same time Chewbacca linked into the sublights, and Solo felt the *Falcon* catch, caught in space, as if trying to determine which way to go, eager to keep running. He nudged her, reversed the throttle on two of the engines, felt the ship yielding, then brought the remaining throttles back up. All at once the tunnel was gone and they were looking at Cyrkon, brown, red, and gold beneath them.

They'd done it flawlessly. The Emperor himself couldn't have complained. Solo actually grinned, forgetting his bad mood for an instant.

Then the *Falcon's* proximity alarm started shrieking, and the bad mood came back as Solo twisted in his seat to silence it.

"What?" he demanded, more of the ship than of his copilot. "What?"

Chewbacca barked, twisting one of the dials on the sensor array, then slapping the aft-view camera to life. Solo stared at the image on the tiny monitor embedded in the control console and tried to keep his jaw from dropping.

"You've got to be kidding me."

Chewbacca snuffed at him, cocking his head.

"Yes, Chewie, I think they see us."

There was a crackle from the speakers in the cockpit, the open communications channel springing to life.

"*This is the Star Destroyer* Vehement." The voice had all the arrogance and entitlement Solo had come to expect from an Imperial officer. *"Unknown YT-1300, identify your-self and state your business on Cyrkon."*

Solo reached for the headset, holding it to one ear as he gestured to Chewie, but he needn't have bothered—his copilot was already half out of his seat, reaching under one of the consoles to his starboard for the case full of ship aliases they used for the *Falcon*. Every ship in the galaxy had, built in as part of its core construc-tion, an identity that was broadcast to other ships that came near enough. Called the Identification Friend or Foe—or IFF—transponder, it was a unique ID, theo-retically impossible to alter, and never mind that it was positively criminal even to try. That hadn't stopped the original owners of the *Falcon* from doing so, and in the intervening years Solo and Chewbacca had built on the already considerable library of aliases for the ship so that now they had, quite literally, hundreds of false names and the documentation to go with them.

"Well, hello there!" Solo said. He discovered that he had affected a definite twang and decided to run with it. "Lovely day, isn't it, *Vehement*?"

Chewie had the case open on his lap and was pull-ing data cubes. He held one up to Solo, looking at him quizzically. Plugged in, it would say the *Falcon* was a ship called *Jin-Den Smoke*, running charter for a family named DeWeir. Solo shook his head.

"*Unknown YT-1300, we repeat, identify and state your business on Cyrkon or you will be boarded. You have ten seconds to comply.*"

"Now that's no way to greet someone," Solo said. Chewie held up another two cubes, one that would say they were the *Broken Bell* carrying hydraulic replacement parts for heavy binary lifters, the other calling them *Foul Matter*, which was carrying—appropriately enough—sanitation supplies. Solo again shook his head, this time more vigorously, and followed it with a look that said, plainly, they didn't have time for this. Chewbacca threw up his hands, dropped the cubes, and rummaged around for more. "You talk that way to all the ships that come across your bow?"

"*Unknown YT-1300, you have five seconds to comply. Broadcast your transponder identification and state your business on Cyrkon.*"

"Now, rein in your eopies," Solo said. "Got it right here. There something going on down there that—"

"Three seconds. Two seconds—"

Chewbacca held up a final cube and, even before Solo could identify it, slammed it home into its receiver on the console, pounding the transmit button at almost the same instant.

"You all should have it now, *Vehement*," Solo said.

There was a pause, nothing but silence over the open channel. Solo and Chewbacca stared at each other. If the identity was rejected—or worse, identified as false—they'd be facing an Imperial Star Destroyer at point-blank range. At best, they *might* be able to evade long enough to make the jump back to light-speed, but the mission would have failed before it had truly begun, never mind that there was already a Star Destroyer orbiting Cyrkon; there was a good chance they'd arrived too late anyway.

"We identify you as Lost and Found, *Captain Coszel Dridge. State your business and cargo."*

"A-yep, that's me," Solo said. "Just heading down to refuel and get a little R and R is all. Understand there's a cantina out on the south side of Motok, you know, the capital, where they have the cutest little Twi'lek dancers you've ever—"

"Your perversions are of no interest to us, Captain Dridge. In future, you are advised to transmit your ship identification immediately upon exiting hyperspace. You are free to go about your business. Vehement out."

There was a click as the communications channel closed.

Solo and Chewbacca slumped back in their seats, exhaling in unison.

The *Falcon* shuddered as it cut through the atmosphere, and settled as Solo and Chewbacca guided her through the toxic skies of Cyrkon on approach to the capital. Chewie keyed in coordinates while Solo finalized their landing arrangements with Motok flight control, securing a landing bay in one of the largest facilities on the edge of the city.

There was good and bad about hiding out on Cyrkon, Solo reasoned. The good was that the local government was as corrupt as the Imperial one, and with enough credits one could bribe or buy one's way to just about anything one needed. While there was, ostensibly, a working economy on the planet, the real business was made on the black market, dealing in goods and weapons and spice and, sometimes, even slaves. If you could make money on it, it was probably being bought or sold in one of Cyrkon's cities.

The bad was that Cyrkon didn't have much in the way of said cities. There was Motok, by far the largest and thus the de facto capital, and perhaps a half dozen others scattered across the planet, but that was it. There was a good reason for this: Cyrkon's cities were all domed, enclosed structures with regulated temperature and atmosphere controls. When the planet had been colonized, long before the fall of the Republic, it had been an ideal, almost idyllic world, situated perfectly in the habitable zone from its single star. Since then, the atmosphere had turned poisonous as industrial and commercial ventures had filled it with toxins. The temperature had skyrocketed, the surface had begun to overheat, and the result was a runaway greenhouse effect that now meant you either lived under a dome or you died, end of story.

Which meant the cities were overcrowded, over-populated, and underserved. Lots of places to hide, sure, but not a lot of places to run.

The *Falcon* glided toward the cluster of port structures as directed by flight control, and Solo brought the ship in a slow pass over their designated bay. Each bay was protected by a magnetic shield—a faint, blue-tinged shimmering of energy—and several were occupied. Chewie leaned forward, peering past him, joining him in a survey of the visible ships parked below. In one of the bays, they could see an Imperial troop transport, *Sentinel* class.

The Wookiee rumbled unhappily.

"Maybe they didn't land a full complement," Solo said.

Chewbacca didn't bother to dignify that with a reply. Instead, he pointed, one hairy finger indicating another ship parked in a bay perhaps half a klick from the Imperial transport. This one wasn't military, not at all, but rather a 1550-LEX, a luxury yacht with a bright blue stripe painted along the top of its hull, running from bow to stern. Chewie snuffed a question at him.

"Looks like her, yeah."

Chewie snuffed a second time, lower.

"We'll see."

Solo flicked the throttles, brought the *Falcon* through a one-eighty that reversed their direction, put them into a hover over their designated landing bay, then set the ship down onto its pad as gently as if he were kissing a child on the nose. Chewie began securing systems and Solo set the engines to standby, as opposed to full shutdown. The Wookiee looked at him.

"Like you don't think we'll be leaving in a hurry," Solo said.

The Wookiee considered, then huffed in agreement. He rose, grabbed his bowcaster from where it rested in the empty navigator's chair behind where he'd been sitting, and looked at Solo again.

"Well, let's hope you won't need it."

They stepped from the cockpit and down the short hall to the circular main compartment. Chewie rumbled, growled, then barked as Solo lowered the ramp and they stepped from the ship and out into the bay.

"I don't know," Solo said. "You can pack a lot of stormtroopers into one of those *Sentinel* shuttles."

That got another chuff in response.

"Look, it's a big city, pal. We don't know if *Vehement*'s after him. It could just be a coincidence, right? And even if they are searching for Ematt, they're gonna be spread out. So we keep our eyes open, we play it smart, we'll be fine. In and out, nobody'll even know we were here."

They started across the landing bay, toward the main doors that led to the port. The Wookiee rumbled again.

"I'm trying to maintain a spirit of optimism, here, Chewie," Solo said. He was getting annoyed. "If you're nervous about this, I'm gonna take this moment to remind you that this was *your* idea. I wanted nothing to do with it, remember?"

The Wookiee woofed as Solo reached the doors and keyed them open. They slid apart, revealing a long, wide, bustling promenade that stretched as far as the eye could see, with more corridors leading to the other bays extending from either side. The noise was immediate—voices arguing, shouting in a dozen languages, speeders whizzing past, droids yammering in binary, vendors hawking their wares from their stalls. They stepped through, and Solo hit the door controls, locking the *Falcon* safely behind them.

"Look, relax," Solo said, turning to face Chewbacca. "We've dealt with stormtroopers before. It could be worse."

The Wookiee rumbled softly.

Solo spun, watching as the crowd parted to reveal an oddly tall and lean figure some fifteen meters away, leading a group of three humanoids. It took another half second before Solo could recognize the leader as a droid, unlike any he'd ever seen. Its face was a mockery of a protocol droid's—flat, matte gray with an extended collar flaring out around it, like some steel flower. Its chassis was humanoid but seemed only partially completed, ending midtorso and revealing the whirling machinery sunk into its waist. Its legs were long, an imitation of human skeletal structure, like its arms. It carried a heavy blaster pistol in one metal fist and a longer, crueler-looking blaster carbine in the other. The three behind the droid, a Kubaz—his long snout visible even from that distance—a Gran, and a human, were likewise moving their weapons into position.

"Han Solo," the droid said, and even across the distance its voice was clear, clipped, metallic like the rest of its form. "Jabba says hello."

Then the droid opened fire.

CHAPTER 04
PRESSING QUESTIONS

"**P**UT THEM AGAINST the wall," Beck ordered. "If any one of them tries anything, kill them."

"Ma'am," the sergeant said, then jerked his arm. "You heard her. Move!"

The stormtroopers were in motion at once, tossing tables aside and grabbing the cantina patrons as they went, throwing them roughly toward the wall at the far side of the room. Protests, weakened by the threat of blaster rifles and Imperial impatience, were voiced, but none with conviction. Beck watched with contempt. It hadn't been a nice cantina to begin with, and she doubted any of the criminal riffraff populating it were that nice, either.

When the squad had finished, there were fourteen patrons against the wall, plus the bartender, his one humanoid server, and a service droid. Beck looked the group over as two of the stormtroopers began patting each one down, her eye clicking softly as she viewed each of them through various spectrums. Three had holdout blasters tucked away. One, an old red-hued Twi'lek, was reaching for his. She drew her blaster and pointed it at his forehead.

"Don't," she said.

The Twi'lek didn't.

Beck waited until the stormtroopers had disarmed the group. Not a one of them, including the droid, had been without a weapon. The pile on the only upright table was substantial, including two vibro-knives, as well as the standard assortment of heavy and light blasters, plus one thermal detonator.

"I'm looking for a man," Beck said. From her pocket she pulled her small holoprojector, keyed it, and brought to life the file image of Ematt, three years out of date at the least. She held it out for all to see. "This man, a human. He is who I want. Not you. The sooner you tell me where to find him, the sooner you can go back to your drinking."

Along the wall, the patrons shifted uneasily, some casting glances at one another, the rest staring at Beck. There was a satisfying fear in their expressions.

"If you do not tell me where I can find him," Beck said, "I'll have you all executed."

The bartender spluttered, then found his voice. He was a Devaronian, one of the two horns rising from the top of his head cracked and missing its point. "You can't do that! We haven't done anything!"

"I'll come up with something."

"The Empire has no authority here!"

Beck sighed, stepping forward until she was scant centimeters from the bartender: he backed so hard against the wall she thought he might try to push his way through it. She smiled at him.

"I am the authority here," she said.

"We haven't seen him." This was the Twi'lek. Beck looked at him, flicking her eye into thermal. Twi'leks normally ran hotter than other humanoids and this one was no exception, but his heat signature was even more elevated than normal for his kind. Fear could do that. Along with the thermal signature, her eye gave her pulse rate and respirations, and all these, used properly, could act as a makeshift lie detector.

"None of us have seen him," the Twi'lek added.

"You're lying." Beck pocketed the projector, turning to head for the door. As she passed the sergeant, she said, "Bring him outside. The rest are free to go."

She stepped out of the bar, into the Motok port, and wrinkled her nose at the assault of different scents. The place was filthy; the people were filthy, human and alien alike. Too many aliens, as far as she was concerned, and you could taste the corruption in the air. The whole planet was corrupt, like so many on the Outer Rim, like so many infected by the Hutts' criminal taint. The Empire was occupied by matters elsewhere, Beck knew, but she sincerely hoped that one day the Emperor's eye would turn toward these unlawful pockets of barely maintained civilization and chaos and bring much-needed order.

She would very much enjoy taking part in such an operation.

The sergeant emerged with four of the troopers, leading the Twi'lek, his hands now in binders behind his back.

"I don't know anything," the Twi'lek said.

"But you're lying. I *know* you're lying." Beck gave him her sweetest smile. "And since I know you're lying, I know you can tell me the truth. There are two ways for that to happen. The easy way is you will just tell me. The hard way involves an interrogation droid and a detention cell aboard my Star Destroyer."

The Twi'lek blanched, his red skin fading to something closer to pink.

"So I think it's an easy choice to make, but then again, I'm not you."

"He wasn't . . . . he wasn't dressed like that," the

Twi'lek muttered. "Not like in the holo, but I saw him, this morning, inside. He wasn't here for long."

"What was he doing?"

"I don't know. He was waiting for someone, I think."

"To meet someone?"

The Twi'lek nodded quickly, making his lekku bounce. "That's what I thought, yeah."

"And did he?"

This time he shook his head with the same vigor, making his head-tails sway. "No, he . . . he kept watching the door, and then he just got up and left, he just left."

"To go where?"

"I don't know, I swear on the Maker I don't know!"

Beck used her eye, checked his vitals again. If anything, the Twi'lek was now more frightened than before, but nothing she could see told her that he was lying. She made a face and turned away, gesturing to the sergeant to release him.

"You're letting me go?" The Twi'lek twisted his head, watching as the sergeant unfastened the binders. He brought his freed hands up, rubbing his wrists. "Thank you! Thank you!"

Beck paused. "You know the man was a rebel?"

"I thought he might be, maybe."

Beck sighed, suddenly tired.

"All rebels and rebel sympathizers are to be shot on sight," she said.

She didn't even have to look at the sergeant, didn't bother to turn around. There was a fraction's pause, then the sound of the sergeant's blaster firing, and a moment later the heavy thump of the Twi'lek hitting the ground.

"Get the body out of the street," Beck told the sergeant, again producing her holoprojector. She tabbed the comm button, and a moment later a miniature and shimmering projection of Captain Hove appeared.

"Commander, any progress?"

"I have a confirmed sighting as of this morning. I want a full detachment brought down immediately. We'll begin a grid search of the city, working out from the port."

Hove's image turned away from the camera, and Beck watched as he relayed her orders to some unseen officer on the *Vehement*'s bridge. He turned back to face her.

"You're certain he's still on planet?"

"You're better equipped to answer that than I, Captain."

"We've had no ships take off from Motok since we arrived."

Beck started to form the word *good*, but something in the way he'd said it made her hold back.

"You sound uncertain, Captain Hove."

"No, Commander. No takeoffs, I assure you."

"But . . . ?"

Hove shifted in the image, pulled at the high collar of his uniform. "There've been a handful of landings, nothing really out of the ordinary. One of them gave us pause, but we let it through."

"Tell me."

"Light freighter, the *Lost and Found*. We cleared it for landing about half an hour ago. Its registration checked out, but it was out of date. I checked after we'd cleared it, and it matches the markings of a ship that was put on the watch list a couple days ago. Some unpleasantness leaving Tatooine, I gather."

"Why didn't you inform me of this earlier?"

"Cyrkon is notorious as a hub for pirates and smugglers, Commander. It's not uncommon for a vessel to use an alias. It wasn't until I checked that I saw it was a known vessel."

"Which bay?"

"I hardly think this matters, Commander. I just wanted to inform—"

"I didn't ask what you think and I certainly don't care, Captain. Which bay?"

Hove, in her palm, looked away, checking something out of sight. "Bay seven thirty-two. But I really don't see—"

Beck jabbed the emitter in her hand, making Hove

vanish midsentence. They were in the eighteen hundreds, with bay seven thirty-two more than a kilometer away.

"They're here to rescue him," she told the sergeant.

She began to run, the clatter of the stormtroopers close at her back.

PART
TWO

CHAPTER 05
MISFORTUNE

"LOOK," SOLO SAID. "Can we talk about this?"

The answer came in the form of another salvo of blaster fire ripping overhead, narrowly skimming the top of the overturned zeezfuruit cart that Solo had taken cover behind. Shards of masonry showered down, pieces of it vaporized into a fine dust that made him sneeze. He glanced to his right, checking on Chewie. The Wookiee had taken cover behind what had once been a shiny and brand-new landspeeder. It was big enough to shield Chewie from the bounty hunters' collective fire, but unfortunately for the vehicle, it had now been hit in a dozen places and its windshield reduced to shards.

That landspeeder's owner was not going to be happy when he or she got back, Solo thought.

The Wookiee was reloading his bowcaster, palming one of the clips from his bandolier and slapping it into place on the weapon. He grunted at Solo.

"I *am* trying to think of something," Solo said.

There was another salvo, and Solo shifted in his crouch. Chewie was watching him—Solo nodded, and both moved at once to return fire. The bounty hunters had similarly gone for cover. The droid was positioned behind one of the heavy support columns along one side of the promenade, but the Gran was, for the moment, exposed. Solo snapped off two shots in quick succession, the first catching the Gran high on the left shoulder, the second missing. The Gran cursed in Huttese.

Chewie roared and Solo heard the bowcaster's distinctive snap, catching in his periphery the flight of the long, slower-moving bolt launched from the weapon. The pillar the droid was hiding behind took the hit, but a significant chunk of the permacrete vaporized.

Solo ducked back down, exhaling and adjusting the DL-44 in his hand. This was not going well. They were wasting time, and with all this shooting, it wouldn't be long before an Imperial parade of bucketheads showed up to investigate the commotion.

Something ominously heavy clattered onto the ground nearby and rolled into view, whining as it approached steadily and rapidly. Without thinking,

Solo lashed out a foot, the toe of his boot catching the metal ball and sending it bouncing off one of the sidewalls of the now nearly deserted promenade. An instant later the ball exploded, and Solo felt a moment's gratitude that this part of the port had cleared almost instantly when the shooting had begun. Bounty hunters came in all shapes and sizes, all of them with their own axes to grind. Some, he knew, were very careful on the job, precise and professional. You could respect people like that, even if you didn't agree with the way they made a living. Others, though, cared about nothing but obtaining their target. If innocents got in the way, well, that was just too bad for those innocents. They were collateral damage, just the cost of doing business. With the firepower these guys were carrying, Solo was certain they fell into the latter category and not the former.

But there was one thing that his experience had taught him was universal to all bounty hunters.

"I've got the money," Solo said. "Listen to me. I have Jabba's money!"

The firing stopped, and Solo snuck one eye clear of the cart, tightening his grip on his blaster pistol. All four of the bounty hunters were still behind cover, but they had heard him and he knew he had their attention.

"I'll give it to you. All of it."

Chewbacca looked at him in amazement. Solo ignored him.

"All of it, it's yours—just let us go."

"Where?" The droid's voice, metallic and ill-modulated.

"It's on my ship. You let me go and get it, I'll bring it to you."

"Solo." The droid sounded disappointed. "If I let you go to the ship, you will not come back. We will come with you."

"You come with us, there's nothing to stop you shooting us in the back once you have the money."

"Correct."

"So you can see why I'd think that's kind of a rotten deal."

"We can offer you another deal," the droid said. "We can kill you here, then take your ship and your money."

"I don't like either deal," Solo said.

Chewie snorted in agreement.

Solo sighed and looked down the promenade in the direction he was facing, away from the bounty hunters.

There was a squad of Imperial stormtroopers approaching, led by an officer with a blaster in her hand. Solo quickly holstered his pistol and looked to Chewie.

"Put it down!" he hissed.

The Wookiee looked at him like he was mad, then in the direction Solo was pointing—and then he got it and promptly put the bowcaster aside.

"Rebels!" Solo shouted, pointing roughly in the direction of the droid.

The bounty hunters chose that moment to resume firing, and the officer and stormtroopers immediately scattered, splitting into two groups and pressing themselves against either side of the promenade. Blaster bolts sailed over Solo's head, smashing into the walls and ground farther down the wide hallway. Solo pushed off from the cart and began running low toward where the officer had taken cover behind another of the pillars. More shots peppered the wall behind him; he felt the heat of one of the bolts singe his hair as he slid in next to her, breathless and not needing to work very hard at pretending to be scared.

"They're crazy!" Solo said to the Imperial officer. "They were going for one of the ships and then something happened—they just started shooting! I think they're trying to escape!"

"Stay back!" the woman said, pushing him against the wall. She was tall, almost his height, a blond with one blue eye and one cybernetic eye, glowing an infernal red and set in a black metal housing fused to her skin. It was frightening to look at. The scar that ran vertically from her hairline to her jaw along that side was deep, and the wound that had made it must've hurt terribly. "How many?"

"Four, I think," Solo said, making his eyes wide. "Two *aliens* and a droid. They're being led by a human."

The officer's jaw clenched and she pivoted, motioning to the troopers in position across the way.

"Set for stun. I want them all alive. We'll need an ion blaster."

"I can help you," Solo said.

"You've done enough, citizen. Stay here where you're safe. I'll want to speak with you once these traitors are in custody."

"My fr—my servant, he's trapped up there." Solo pointed to where Chewbacca was still hunched down behind the damaged landspeeder. "I need him. He's very expensive to replace."

"We'll clear the route," the officer said. She motioned again to the troopers opposite her, giving them the go signal. They moved the way stormtroopers always moved: quickly and precisely and as a unit, advancing in groups, giving one another support fire, making their way quickly up the promenade. The bounty hunters were shooting back, either unwilling to surrender their bounty to the Empire or, more likely, not yet realizing that the battle they were fighting had changed, that they were no longer exchanging shots with Solo and Chewbacca.

The group reached the landspeeder, and Chewbacca scooped up his bowcaster and ran in long-legged strides to where Solo was waiting for him. They each spared a glance back up the promenade.

"This is Commander Beck of the Imperial Security Bureau," Solo heard the woman shouting. *"Throw down your weapons and surrender and your lives will be spared!"*

Chewie huffed.

"Definitely time for us to go," Solo agreed.

The cantina was in a cargo hold, and the cargo hold was in the 1550-LEX they'd seen on approach. It had taken only a moment to double-check that the ship was the one Solo and Chewie thought it was, *Miss Fortune*. They slipped into the docking bay without difficulty and without anyone paying them any attention. They approached from the back of the vessel, where the cargo ramp was down and a very taciturn Shistavanen was leaning against one of the hydraulic struts. They could hear music and voices coming from within. The Shistavanen held up a clawed paw, stopping them.

"Cover is fifteen credits," he growled. He raised his lupine head, muzzle canted up to look Chewbacca in the eyes. "Twenty for the Wook."

"I'm a friend of Delia's," Solo said.

"Everyone's a friend of Delia's," the Shistavanen said. "Thirty-five credits, buddy."

"Robbery," Solo told Chewbacca, fishing the chits out of one of his pockets. He dropped them into the Shistavanen's hand. "Don't spend it all in one place."

They climbed the ramp into what had once been the substantial and reasonably spacious cargo hold of the ship. Technically, Solo supposed it still was the cargo hold of the ship, but that was no longer the purpose of the space, nor had it been for a very long time. Instead, there was a long bar top against the fore-end bulkhead, with transparent cases behind it displaying bottles and bottles of the finest liquors the galaxy had to offer. A half dozen small round-top tables filled the rest of the space, with two or sometimes three seats at each—and most were occupied.

The freight that got moved aboard *Miss Fortune* was primarily liquid in form, frequently intoxicating, and generally overpriced, but it came with the benefit of being served in just about the most discreet location possible. *Miss Fortune* needed no permits, paid no taxes, and, when the local authorities got wind of those two facts, could quite literally pick up and fly away at a moment's notice to set down on some other world and repeat the process all over again. For people who made their living on the go, traveling from world to world—smugglers, scouts, mercenaries—it was the perfect place to have a safe and quiet drink and maybe catch up on the latest news.

Solo led the way to the bar, threading between the tables and bellying up between two empty stools. The bartender, facing away from him, was a human woman with short red hair. When she turned and saw him, a grin broke across her pale, lightly freckled face. Then Solo realized she wasn't looking at him, but at Chewbacca.

"Hey, Wookiee," the woman said, pushing up on tiptoe and leaning out to wrap Chewie in a hug. Chewbacca chuffed, embracing her and lifting her off her feet, and Solo saw her cheeks color nearly the shade of her hair as she was squeezed.

"You're gonna break Delia, Chewie," Solo said.

Chewbacca rumbled, barked once, and set her back down. The woman steadied herself and ran fingers through her hair, catching her breath.

"Solo," she said. She was trying not to wheeze.

"Captain Leighton."

Delia Leighton grinned again. "I heard you were dead, Han. I heard that Greedo splattered you all over Mos Eisley or something like that. I was almost sad about it."

"Almost?"

"You still haven't paid your tab."

"I've got the money."

"That so?" She put her elbows on the bar, lines crinkling at the corners of her eyes as she smiled. "Let's see it."

"I don't have it with me."

"I knew you'd say that."

"I can pay you. The money's on the *Falcon*." Solo leaned closer, putting the two of them face-to-face. "That and more if you can maybe help us out."

"Always an angle with you."

"No angle, just information. I'm looking for someone."

"We're all looking for someone, Solo." Delia straightened, pulled the hand towel from where it hung, tail stuffed into the belt at her waist, and began wiping down the bar. An old WA-7 series droid rolled up on her single wheel and set her tray on the bar.

"Two juri, an incandescent, and one bottle of Bost," the droid said.

Delia began filling the order.

"Delia, we're in a bit of a hurry," Solo said.

"And that's new how?"

"Can you help us?"

She set a bottle on the tray and popped the cap off. "You haven't told me who you're looking for yet."

"Human male, roughly twenty standard years, brown hair, brown eyes. He would've just arrived in Motok within the last eighteen hours or so."

"So, maybe a third of the humans visiting Motok, that's who you're looking for?" She set two glasses on the waitress's tray, then reached back for a bottle without bothering to look at it, flipped it over her head into her other hand, thumbed the stopper, and began to pour. The liquid that flowed out shimmered, turned silver, and ended up frothing clear in the glasses and smelling like sweet fruit. "You're being uncharacteristically vague."

"He's looking to get off-planet. He's expecting a lift." Solo leaned in once more, catching the bartender's gaze. "He's expecting a very specific lift from some very specific *friends*. The kind of friends you've been known to be sympathetic to."

To her credit, Delia didn't immediately react—just finished filling the order and watched as the droid scooped the tray up and rolled quickly away. She waited, then slowly slid her eyes back to Solo. The suspicion in them was unmistakable.

"You've never been known to stick your neck out for anyone but yourself," she said.

"I'm his ride, Delia."

"I don't believe you."

"You think I'm working for the Empire?"

She glanced at Chewbacca, who had remained silent, listening. She shook her head.

"But there are other people you're known to work for," Delia said. "The slugs."

"I wouldn't sell my worst enemy to the Hutts."

"We both know that's not true."

"Okay," Solo said. "Maybe my *worst* enemy. But that's not this. I'm this guy's lift, Delia."

"I'm supposed to believe you've joined the underground?"

Solo shook his head. "No, no way, absolutely not. This is a one-time thing."

Delia bit her lower lip. "Chewie?"

The Wookiee nodded.

"Straight-up?"

The Wookiee nodded again and huffed.

She shook her head slightly, amazed.

"They must be paying you an awful lot," Delia said.

"Not nearly enough," Solo said.

CHAPTER 06

CAPTIVATING

"EXECUTE, SIGMA FOUR," the stormtrooper sergeant ordered. Instantly, two of the soldiers flanking either side of the promenade were in motion, a run-and-gun that they'd drilled so many times it required no thought to put into action: advancing, firing, advancing.

Past the cover of the half-destroyed landspeeder, Beck watched as one of their four opponents went down—the Kubaz, hit twice in quick succession by stun blasts. The remaining three seemed to hesitate, as if stunned by the precision and speed of the attack, and the second team of stormtroopers opened fire then, downing the Gran. The human, his clothing a mixture of salvaged military and refugee, all bundled beneath a filthy cloak, turned and tried to run.

"Stop him," Beck said.

She needn't have spoken at all. The human hadn't made it four strides before he was shot in the back twice in quick succession. His body lit a sudden blue, suffusing him with charged particles that overloaded his nervous system all at once. Through her cybernetic eye, she watched as the human's biosigns went wild for an instant, then collapsed to baseline as the electrical impulses that drove his brain were suddenly and savagely forced into reset by the shock to his system. It was the same process that allowed medical anesthetics to do their job, Beck knew, but somehow, watching it happen to a fleeing rebel made it that much more satisfying.

That left the droid, some leftover model from before the Clone Wars from the looks of it, and it was crab-stepping out of its cover and raising its weapons in some mockery of surrender.

"Do not shoot," the droid said.

The stormtrooper sergeant brought up the short-barreled DEMP gun from its strap over his arm and shot. The electromagnetic pulse hit the droid and the machine locked, trembled, sparks flying in all directions as the ionized charge raced over its housing and through its circuits. The droid made a pathetic, almost childlike whine, then collapsed with a loud clank.

"Efficient," Beck said. It was quite possibly the highest praise she could imagine giving.

The stormtrooper sergeant, designation TX-828, inclined his head ever so slightly in acknowledgment of the compliment. "Thank you, ma'am."

Beck slid her duty blaster back into its holster on her thigh and strode forward. On either side of the promenade, shapes began to appear, those people who had exercised the better part of valor and gone into hiding when the firefight had begun. Shutters slid back on the shops, one after the other, and the whir and whine of droids going into motion melted into background noise as, slowly, communication and then commerce resumed. People stared at her and the stormtroopers as they advanced, the sergeant directing his troopers to disarm and bind the prisoners. Beck ignored them all, focused on the slumped, motionless form of the human lying on the ground, his body now almost entirely concealed by his cloak.

She stopped, standing over him, then used the toe of her boot to nudge his body. For an instant she saw, instead, the Rodian woman who had taken her own life. The anger returned, and it made Beck push harder, forcing the unconscious human onto his back.

"I've been waiting for this a long time, Ematt," Beck said.

The man she was looking at wasn't Ematt.

She looked him over, assessing. The hodgepodge of salvaged military gear and pieces of body armor was recognizable as late-era clone trooper and mock Mandalorian. The weapon in his hand had been dropped, but her cybernetic eye immediately matched it to a schematic—a Merr-Sonn 4, normally used by police for its ability to switch between automatic blaster fire and semiautomatic stun. The hilt of a vibro-blade hung from his belt and a second weapon—a BlasTech HSB-200 holdout, her eye told her—rested in a holster beneath his arm. Three grenades on the belt, two of them stunners.

Beck bent, took hold of the unconscious human by his collar, and searched him with her free hand. He had a pouch beneath his shirt, sensor shielded. She snapped it free from its cord, dropped the man, opened it, and dumped the contents into her palm. Credits, a holoprint, and an ID card. She glared at the card, then threw it down before striding back in the direction she'd come.

"Bounty hunters." She said the words as though each was toxic. "They're bounty hunters, not rebels."

She stopped short, glaring down the once-again bustling promenade.

"The other two, the human and the Wookiee, where'd they go?"

TX-828, the sergeant, said, "I don't see them. They must have run off when we moved on the targets."

"We were just played." Beck felt the fury racing along her spine and fought to control it. "They played us. Those two, those two were the rebels. They're here to rescue Ematt—I'd bet anything on it."

Behind her, she heard the droid grinding back onto its feet. It whirred, clicked, then spoke as she turned to face it.

"This unit is designated Captivator," the droid said. "This unit carries an authorized Imperial certification to hunt bounties. You have interfered with this unit and its partners."

Beck moved closer. "If you have a complaint, droid, file it with the Guild."

"The Imperial officer misunderstands." Something inside the droid's head made a whizzing noise, then settled into a hum that, Beck suspected, was designed to be exactly as annoying as it sounded. "The individuals are not rebels. The individuals are smugglers. The human is designated Solo, Han. The Wookiee is designated Chewbacca. The reward for their acquisition is . . . significant."

"Acquisition."

"It is more significant if they are acquired alive."

Beck looked the droid over, then at the others, the Kubaz and the Gran and the human, all of whom had reached various stages in their return to consciousness.

The Gran, she noted, had been wounded, but it didn't look serious.

"Captivator," Beck said. "Let's talk."

"This unit operates under self-actualization programming." Captivator rotated on its central axis, turning its torso in a full three-sixty while its legs and head remained motionless. Its eyes, such as they were, flickered between yellow and white. Beck felt like the machine was staring at her. "This unit has a self-improvement directive. This unit has acquired programming and modifications to make it the most efficient hunter in the galaxy."

"And an ego modification, I see," Beck said.

"This unit has no ego. This unit relays facts."

"So you're saying you can track those two, Solo and the Wookiee?"

"That is correct."

Beck looked over the rest of Captivator's crew. Now that they had recovered, she didn't know what to make of them. The Kubaz, his long snout dangling from within his hood, whispered something to the human and the Gran, neither of whom had stopped staring at her since the discussion began. The droid was clearly the leader of the team, and knowing what she did about bounty hunters and how they worked, Beck suspected that there was some truth to what Captivator was telling her.

She had ordered the whole group pulled into the relative privacy of one of the small shops lining the promenade, then directed the sergeant to clear the space. It had been a restaurant, alien-focused fast food, and the smell of grease was heavy, mixing with spices from worlds Beck had likely never heard of, let alone visited. The human proprietor watched them suspiciously from the far corner, under guard of another two stormtroopers. Beck considered what she knew.

"You can identify their ship?" she asked the droid.

"Confirmed."

"Do you know where it is?"

"Negative." Captivator clicked. A line of lights on its torso flashed. "But it will be a simple matter for myself and my partners to locate it."

"I want a description of that ship," Beck said. "Its name. Its *real* name, not whatever alias it may have used to land."

The bounty hunters, arrayed behind Captivator, shifted uncertainly, exchanging glances.

"Cannot comply," Captivator said.

"Not only *can* you comply, you *will* comply," Beck said. "Or your next job will be on Kessel, and your partners will find themselves toiling in an Imperial penal colony. Name, description. Now."

A new light flashed on the droid's torso, followed by a gentle hydraulic whine as it rotated its head this time, turning it in a one-eighty to view its partners. The move, Beck suspected, was for show; Captivator sported almost a dozen cameras and lenses on its head. She was certain the droid could see in every direction at once, with the processing power to assess and analyze the information acquired from its sensors near instantly. It was stalling for time.

"Sergeant," Beck said. "Take them into custody on a charge of obstruction and suspicion of aiding and abetting terrorists."

"Yes, ma'am." The stormtrooper raised his right hand, signaling the rest of the squad.

"Wait," Captivator said. Its head swiveled back to face her. "We are loyal to the Empire. We will comply."

The sergeant glanced at Beck, and she nodded, barely. He motioned the squad back.

"I'm waiting."

"The vessel is a KLT-Kuat light freighter," Captivator said. "Vessel is named *Roundabout Right*."

Beck smiled. "Anything else?"

"The vessel is easily identifiable by the depiction of a deep-space Angel painted on its port hull."

Beck stared into the droid's visual sensors. The bounty hunters shifted; she saw the Kubaz creeping one hand ever so slowly toward the blaster holstered at his hip.

"You and your partners are free to go," Beck said.

The droid buzzed. The bounty hunters at its back relaxed. The Kubaz's hand went back to rest at his side.

"Long live the Emperor," Captivator said, then pivoted and headed out of the little café, the other bounty hunters in tow.

The sergeant waited until the door had closed before he said, "Ma'am, I believe they were lying."

"I know they were lying." She faced the proprietor, who hadn't moved. He was roughly the right height, a little overweight, but he would do. "*Vehement* recorded no KLTs landing since they arrived. We're looking for a YT-1300. You, the Empire requires your clothes."

The proprietor opened his mouth to protest, then remembered the two stormtroopers guarding him. He unfastened his apron and began pulling off his tunic.

"Get out of your armor and put those on," Beck told the sergeant. "Take a comlink and follow them. Stay in contact."

"At once, ma'am." It sounded to her like the sergeant was smiling.

"I'll take the rest of the squad and we'll locate their ship. With luck, we'll ambush them as they try to board." She turned back to the proprietor, now standing in his undergarments, and took the bundle of clothes being presented to her by one of the stormtroopers. She set them down on one of the small tabletops. The sergeant was already out of his helmet and gloves, quickly working the fasteners on his breast-plate. He was older than she'd have suspected, perhaps nearing forty, gray beginning to color his black hair. With some surprise Beck realized that he was a clone, perhaps one of the last still in service based on the original Kamino-produced template. That confirmed her suspicions about his age. There were only a few of his kind left. In fact, Beck couldn't remember having ever served alongside one before.

"TX-828," Beck said.

"Yes, Commander?" He was out of his armor, now, pulling on the shirt. His voice sounded strange without the modulation of his helmet.

"What do they call you?"

"Ma'am?" he tucked in his shirt and took the com-link one of his troopers handed him.

"You have a nickname. In the barracks. What do they call you?"

"Torrent, ma'am."

"You'll use that as your call sign." She knelt, pulled the cuff free from her right boot, and detached the small holster and holdout blaster she wore there. She rose again and put the holster with the weapon in Torrent's hand. "For the Empire."

"For the Empire, ma'am."

She watched as he stepped out of the café, checked the street briefly, then disappeared into the bustle of traffic, moving quickly to catch up with Captivator and the rest of the bounty hunters. She turned to one of the troopers, already gathering Torrent's things.

"Let's find that ship," she told him.

CHAPTER 07

DESPERATE MEANS,
IN FULL MEASURE

DELIA LEIGHTON knew trouble when she saw it, a necessary skill as a starship captain and arguably more important as a bartender.

Trouble was on the cargo ramp right now, in the form of four individuals—one droid and three humanoids—arguing with her partner, copilot, and bouncer, Curtis. She reached under her side of the bar top, beside the sink, and put her hand on the grip of the sawed-off Scattermaster she kept hidden there.

"Let them in, Curtis," she called.

The Shistavanen looked at her unhappily, lips curling back along the sides of his muzzle, baring his teeth. She smiled. She always smiled when she could manage it. She'd learned the trick back before she'd acquired the ship, while working as a barmaid in a cantina on Lothal. That had been a rough crowd: spacers and smugglers and pirates, all the different species the galaxy seemed to have to offer coming through at one point or another, including one old Duro who always drank by himself in the corner and told her stories when things got quiet. She'd learned the smile, the friendly demeanor, how to spend hours on her feet—and how to deal with trouble, how to know when it was time to stand your ground, time to hide behind a table, and time to run.

Miss Fortune had been that Duro's ship. He'd left it to her in his will, much to her surprise. Its original name, in Durese, translated to "serendipity," but since Delia could hardly pronounce the Durese and nobody else could pronounce it at all, she'd rechristened it. Suddenly a captain and still a barmaid, she'd combined the two professions. It let her travel, and it let her meet people. Curtis had joined her early. Curtis, who had more sympathy than sense when it came to things like the Rebellion against the Empire. Curtis, who convinced Delia to sometimes let *Miss Fortune* be used to pass messages between rebel cells.

The group made their way up the ramp, the droid leading. They had weapons in hand, though not raised. The few patrons at the tables carefully picked up their drinks and moved out of the way. The WA-7, Bobbie, swiveled in place, tray perfectly balanced on her hand, and watched them pass.

"Get you fellas a drink?" Bobbie asked, voice modulator flashing as she spoke.

The four ignored her and approached the bar.

"I'm afraid we're not equipped to serve droids," Delia said. She was still smiling.

The droid rotated in place, its head, then torso spinning twice quickly to take in the bar before stopping as quickly as it had begun. One of its optical sensors came to life, glowing blue, and an instant later a beam of the same color lanced out, scanning Delia from head to toe.

"That's a little rude," Delia said. Her smile never faltered.

"There was a Wookiee here," the droid said. "Analysis of the local atmosphere detects dander. Optical analysis detects the presence of three Wookiee hairs on your clothes. You had close contact with him."

She tightened her grip on the shotgun beneath the bar, but kept the smile in place.

"Who's asking?" she said.

"The Wookiee traveled with a human, a Corellian. Name Solo, Han. Verify."

"Who's asking?" Delia said a second time.

The weapons came up, and came up quickly, and suddenly Delia was looking at the wrong end of five blasters. The Gran at the droid's right slammed his fist on the bar. "We're asking!"

"If your hand's on a weapon, little lady, I'd let it go and take a step back," the human said.

"Verify," the droid repeated.

Curtis had come off the ramp and was now approaching slowly and quietly from behind the group. Delia tried to catch his eye, to warn him off, but either he didn't see her or he didn't listen. From his belt he pulled the grip of his shockstaff, the one he used when customers sometimes got out of hand, and moved a clawed thumb over the activation stud. The weapon extended in both directions instantly, locking into position as a quarterstaff, a glow of energy surging at either end.

The droid's torso spun. Delia moved to free the shotgun, but the Gran and the human both leapt forward, grabbing her by each arm. Curtis got as far as midleap, the staff raised to come down on the droid, and then there was a single shot.

Delia Leighton lost her smile. "No!"

Curtis hit the deck hard, growling. He tried to get up, and the droid shot him again. This time the stun bolt took, and Delia watched, her arms now gripped by the human and the Gran, as her friend collapsed, the staff rolling from his hand.

"Get him," the droid said.

The last of the four, the Kubaz, bent and yanked

Curtis to his feet, wrapping one arm beneath the Shistavanen's neck.

"Put your blaster to his head," Captivator said.

The Kubaz looked at the droid, gurgled at him.

"If we do not complete this bounty within the allotted time, there will be further complications." The droid's head swiveled, primary optics focusing on the Kubaz. "We do not want to compete with Boba Fett."

The Kubaz gurgled again in agreement and with his free hand put his blaster to Curtis's jaw.

"My colleague will kill the Shistavanen if you do not verify." The droid's torso swiveled back, weapons again pointed at Delia. "Verify."

"They were here," Delia said. "Let him go!"

"Insufficient. Time since present."

"Not long, less than an hour." She watched as the Kubaz pushed the barrel of his blaster harder into the side of Curtis's neck, crushing the fur there. "Please, let him go."

"Where are they now?"

Delia hesitated. Curtis whined softly in the back of his throat, eyes opening. He was staring at her.

"They went into the city," Delia said. "They were going shopping."

The droid hummed to itself for a moment. "This unit is equipped with a biomedical sensor array and voice analysis suite that will accurately detect false-hoods. You are lying."

"I'm not, I'm—"

The droid's head swiveled to face the Kubaz, acting as if it was looking at him. "In five seconds, kill the Shistavanen."

Delia strained against the hands holding her, heart racing near to panic. "No! No, I'm telling the truth!"

"Four seconds."

"Please—"

"Three."

"Please, listen—"

"Two."

"They went to meet someone!" she blurted, desperation making her shout. "They had to meet someone!"

The droid's head swiveled back to look at her.

"Location."

She felt like she wanted to cry, suddenly, could feel the ache behind her eyes. She sagged in the grip on her arms. Curtis was looking at her, yellow eyes wide, begging her not to betray the rebels.

She didn't have a choice.

She told them everything.

CHAPTER 08
WOOKIEE POWERED,
REBELLION APPROVED

THE ONLY THING that made Motok different from a thousand other cities in the Outer Rim that Han Solo had visited at one time or another was, as far as he could tell, the presence of the dome. And even that wasn't unique. It was just another city, founded by colonists who'd ventured out from the Core Worlds in search of opportunity and a better life. It had grown, it had flourished, it had faced setbacks, it had built a dome, and life had gone on and ever on, as it did. There were people in Motok who were born, lived, and would die without ever leaving the dome, without ever knowing what it was to breathe fresh air or feel natural weather, rain or snow or the kiln-dry heat of a desert world. Solo felt a little sorry for those people. The galaxy was a big place, the universe a bigger one; it seemed a waste of a life not to try to taste at least some of the feast that was out there.

They'd rented a speeder—one of the new V-40s—at the port, and Chewie didn't approve of the choice, mostly because the vehicle hadn't been built with Wookiees in mind. It was a little on the flashy side, a slate gray with black flarings and a convertible top, but Solo hadn't picked it for those features. It would be fast, and he knew the Imperials would be after them soon enough, if not already. Speed, as it had been so many times before for him, was a crucial ally. It wasn't cheap, either, but he figured they had the credits to burn, and anyway, he'd bill Her Royal Annoyance and the Rebel Alliance for it once they'd made the rendezvous.

Solo programmed the in-dash navicomp and set a destination near the location Delia had given them. He was still a little annoyed at her reluctance to believe he was working with the rebels, then found himself wondering why he cared what she thought of him, anyway. It irked him only slightly more that she'd looked to Chewie for confirmation, that his word hadn't been good enough. Sure, there were times when Solo lied, there were times when he cheated, there were times when he played fast and loose—but never with his friends.

"I'm a trustworthy guy," he said to Chewbacca, out of the blue. "I mean, you can trust me, right?"

The Wookiee shifted in the seat beside him, his knees nearly tucked beneath his chin, still trying to get comfortable. He let out a low collection of rumbles, punctuated with a bark.

"That's different," Solo said. "You know that's different. Dealing with people like Jabba, you've got to stay on your toes. Those types, they're always looking to put one over on us. It's a question of doing it to them before they do it to us."

Chewbacca growled, barked softly again.

"Name one time. Name one."

The Wookiee rumbled and began speaking. After thirty seconds or so, Solo cut him off.

"You've made your point."

Chewie chuckled.

"We came back to help the kid."

A snort.

"That was not all about a reward."

Another snort.

"The princess trusted me enough to ask us to do this."

Chewie smoothed the fur covering his knees and looked at Solo. The Wookiee barked.

"Okay, fine, she trusted us both. So did Delia."

Chewie just shook his head and growled gently. Solo guided the speeder off the main drag and down a narrowing side street. Buildings were getting shorter, the neighborhood clearly turning more downscale, with faulty lighting and fewer pedestrians.

"Yeah," Solo said, more to himself than his friend. "Yeah, they trust you, not me—you're right."

The navicomp chimed, and Solo pulled the landspeeder over, parking it around the corner from the address Delia had provided. He and Chewie took a moment to check the street and saw it was all but deserted, with the exception of a municipal service droid vainly fighting a losing battle against litter. Solo pulled himself up and swung his legs over the edge of the speeder. Chewie took longer, snarling to himself.

"Stop complaining," Solo said. "Next time I'll pick something bigger, okay?"

They rounded the corner, headed down the block. A sign ahead of them flickered with faulty wiring, alternately telling them that there was vacancy or not, depending on when the circuits cut out. The doors to the hotel slid apart as they approached, one of them sticking, forcing Chewbacca not only to bend his head to clear the top of the doorframe but also to turn sideways. Solo led the way through the lobby, ignoring the droid clerk behind the counter. It wasn't the lowest rent hotel Solo had visited, but he wouldn't recommend it to his friends. An old human was asleep on a bench beside the elevators, but he woke up enough to yawn and stare at them as they waited for the car.

"Your friend needs a shave," the man said.

"Never heard that one before." Solo reached into a pocket, pulled a couple of credits, and held them out. "You want to make a little change?"

"Depends what I have to do."

"You see anyone coming through here who looks like they don't belong, you hit the environment alert. You do that for me?"

"You mean anyone aside from him?" The man indicated Chewbacca.

"You know what I mean."

The old man eyed the chits in Solo's palm. "I can do that."

"You're a credit to our species," Solo told him.

They came off the elevator and into a dimly lit hall, the scent of old food and sweat strong in the air. Chewie eased the strap for his bowcaster off his shoulder and moved the weapon into his hands, checking in both directions as Solo moved forward, reading the numbers on the doors. Solo's right hand dropped to his holster and unsnapped the strap holding his blaster in place. The Wookiee made an almost inaudible woof.

"Yeah, pal," Solo said. "Me too."

They reached the door to the room Delia had given them. There was a doorbell, but Solo ignored it; Delia had told him to knock. He rapped his knuckles once beneath the eye slit. "Here for a pickup," he said. "Package from Alderaan."

There was silence. Behind him, Solo could sense Chewie checking the hall, covering his back.

"I remember Alderaan," a voice said from the other side of the door.

"Never forget," Solo said.

The magnetic locks on the door slid back with a solid *thunk*.

"Come in," the voice said.

Solo shared a look with Chewie, then tabbed the OPEN button on the panel above the doorbell. The door slid open immediately, revealing a room narrower than the hall itself and even more poorly lit. A single fixture, recessed into the wall on the left, guttered, then flared bright for a moment, and in it Solo could see a man, dressed in refugee attire, tears in his tunic and poncho. He looked to be in his mid-twenties at most, and like a man who was living on a cocktail of suspicion, fatigue, and worry. His hands were out of sight beneath the poncho, and Solo had a very good idea what they were holding.

"Close it behind you," the man said.

Solo stepped inside far enough to allow Chewie to enter behind him. The door closed with a whine, and the one ceiling light flicked on, dropping a blue-white glare onto all of them.

"Who're you?"

"Han Solo. I'm captain of the *Millennium Falcon*." Solo jerked a thumb back toward Chewbacca, looming over his shoulder. "This is Chewbacca, my partner."

The man looked at them, then brought his hands out, empty, from where they'd been hidden. "Ematt. You're my ride?"

"We're your ride. Sooner we're out of here the better."

"No argument."

The lights suddenly changed hue, flashing red. An instant later, a klaxon started blaring. Ematt started, one hand again vanishing beneath the poncho, this time emerging with a blaster carbine, its barrel cut down, presumably for ease of concealment. He stared at them accusingly.

"You bring the Empire with you?"

"Not on purpose." Solo swore, turning and drawing his pistol.

Chewie had opened the door and was sticking his head out, bowcaster at the ready. The Wookiee growled back at Solo over his shoulder.

"Chewie says it's clear. We should move."

"Stairs at the end of the hall," Ematt said. "Safer than the lift."

"You heard the man," Solo said.

Chewie led, long legs taking him down the hall quickly enough that Solo and Ematt had to run to keep up. They reached the door to the stairs and the Wookiee hit the panel, but the door refused to open. Chewie slapped a hand against the panel a second time, and there was a whining noise. On the display above it, Solo could read the words EMERGENCY LOCKOUT.

"Environmental emergency," Solo muttered. Of course the building sealed itself off.

"Elevator," Ematt hissed.

"Get it open!" Solo told Chewbacca, turning back toward the elevators and pressing his side against the wall. Ematt, on the opposite side of the hall, was mirroring the maneuver, bringing up his carbine. Behind him came the sound of metal tearing as Chewie tore the door panel's access plate free from the wall and began yanking at wires.

"Don't hotwire it! Open it!"

Chewie snarled, and Solo thought it better not to respond—all the more so since that was the moment the elevator chimed and its doors opened to reveal the same droid from the port. It whirled into view, planting itself squarely and bringing up both its guns. From the corner of his eye, Solo could see Ematt glaring at him.

"On the bright side," Solo said, "they're not Imperials."

"Then who are they?" Ematt demanded.

"Bounty hunters."

The droid opened fire, ripping plaster chunks off the wall over Solo's head.

"Bounty hunters?" Ematt sounded incredulous. "You let bounty hunters follow you?"

"I didn't *let* them do anything!" Solo snapped off two shots, both hits. Neither seemed to bother the droid much at all, because it immediately returned fire. "Delia sold us out! It's not my fault!"

Behind him, Chewie roared in fury, and Solo twisted around in time to see that the Wookiee had abandoned trying to rewire the panel and now had both hands wedged in the seam of the door to the stairwell. He roared again, louder, and the door suddenly broke apart with a gratifying sound of rending metal. Chewie looked at him, satisfied.

"Yes, you're very strong—go!" Solo gestured to Ematt. "Go!"

Ematt loosed three shots of suppressing fire from his carbine in quick succession, and Solo followed those with another four from his pistol. With a lunge, Ematt was off the wall and through the door, Chewie after him. Solo laid down another salvo, then followed the others into the stairwell. Chewie was somehow again in the lead, leaping from landing to landing ahead of them, bowcaster gripped in one fist. Ematt clambered down the steps after him, with Solo on his tail, checking over his shoulder. For a handful of seconds there was nothing but the sound of their movement as they descended as quickly as possible, and then a blaster shot rang out from above and shattered the concrete a bare centimeter from Solo's left foot. He fired back, up the stairwell, without looking.

The sound of a Wookiee's snarl filled the space, echoing, and Solo looked down, past Ematt. Chewie had reached the bottom of the stairs. The Kubaz bounty hunter had anticipated this escape route and was trying to cut them off. Solo pushed past Ematt and raised his blaster, trying to find a shot, but the angle was horrible. Chewie and the Kubaz were too close to each other for Han to risk it. The Wookiee roared again and with one hand lifted the Kubaz by the front of his shirt and smashed him against the wall. Then Chewbacca tossed him through the now-open doors into the lobby.

"Okay," Ematt said. "He's strong."

"Move," Solo said.

They emerged into the lobby, the old man still on his bench. "I did what you asked." He held out a palm. Solo flipped some credits at the old man and ran through the lobby, Ematt beside him. Chewie was now behind them, and Solo once again heard the distinctive snap of the bowcaster firing, the bass thud of the shot smashing into a wall. Higher-pitched blaster fire chased them out into the street, and Solo turned to head for the speeder, catching movement off to his right. The human had taken position behind what Solo intuited was the bounty-hunting team's own speeder. Solo lashed a hand back to grab Ematt's poncho and pulled him down as he dove. The human's shot sizzled overhead and punched a dent in the facade of the hotel.

"They're not using stun," Solo said. Then, more indignantly, "They're trying to kill us!"

The Wookiee reached down and yanked Solo back to his feet, Solo in turn pulling Ematt up after him. Chewie whuffed.

"Alive," Solo said. "We're worth more alive!"

"Less talk, more run," Ematt said.

They made the corner and turned it as another shot narrowly skimmed past Solo's shoulder. A swoop bike was parked a half-dozen meters short of where Solo had left the speeder. It hadn't been there before, and he nearly smashed into it. He twisted and kept running for the V-40. Solo vaulted into the speeder's front seat, thankful he'd left the top down, and Ematt similarly tumbled into the passenger seat beside him. The vehicle sagged on its repulsors as Chewie dove into the back. Solo kicked the engine to life, slammed the throttle forward, and wrenched the yoke, and the speeder shot forward and slewed into a one-eighty. Ahead of them, now, the human was standing in the open and raising his rifle to his shoulder. The weapon was scoped, and Solo could swear he felt the reticle on him, the crosshairs settling between his eyes. The speeder howled, launching toward the man.

Solo realized he was about to get shot. There was nothing he could do, no place to move the speeder, no other direction to turn. The human had him dead to rights.

Beside him, Ematt was on one knee in his seat. Raising his own carbine to his shoulder, he fired. Solo was certain he'd missed, but the human bounty hunter staggered and fell, his own shot going wild. The speeder tore forward as Solo brought it through the turn, accelerating back in the direction of the hotel. They flew past the entrance just as the Gran and the droid emerged. Chewie fired once, the bowcaster's bolt exploding over the bounty hunters' heads, then ducked down to avoid return fire. Solo, on the rear-screen projection, saw the Gran go down, pelted by rubble. The droid loosed a salvo at them, one of the bolts skipping off the tail of the speeder. The vehicle dipped, and Solo jerked the yoke and brought it back under control.

"I hope you have a plan," Ematt said.

"Yes, we have a plan," Solo said. "We go to the port, we go to our ship, we leave. That's the plan. It's a good plan."

"It's not a very good plan."

"I can take you back to your hotel if you'd like," Solo said.

"No, thank you," Ematt said. "We'll try your plan."

Solo swung the speeder onto the main drag and opened the throttle to full. Buildings and vehicles blurred past. He checked the rear screen again, catching his breath. Chewbacca was reloading.

"She sold us out," Solo said.

The Wookiee snarled angrily.

"Then how else did they know where to find us?" Solo demanded.

"I can think of a couple of ways," Ematt said, settling back in his seat. "Betrayal isn't the only option."

"Yeah, well, it's the one I'm used to."

"I feel sorry for you, then. Trust is as precious as it is rare, but you only get it by giving it."

Ematt was sounding an awful lot like the old man had.

"Trust isn't given, it's earned," Solo said. "Like friendship."

"You must be very lonely," Ematt said.

Solo didn't respond.

PART
THREE

CHAPTER 09
NO MISTAKES, NO ESCAPES

"THAT'S THE SHIP," Beck said.

"Yes, ma'am." The stormtrooper beside her, a corporal now commanding the squad in Torrent's place, sounded dubious, even through the speakers on his helmet. "It doesn't look like much, ma'am."

Beck nodded slightly, agreeing. The ship was a YT-1300, as Captain Hove had reported. To her eye the ship hadn't seen a good day since it came off the Corellian Engineering line all those years ago. Paint seemed an afterthought to its owners, and the innumerable dents and scratches along the hull made the ship look not as much used as abused.

Another of the squad stepped up and pointed a handheld scanner at the vessel, taking a quick reading from stem to stern. "They've modified the IFF transponder," the trooper said. "Lot of noise. Can't get a positive ID. It's broadcasting as *Lost and Found*."

"Take its silhouette and send it up to *Vehement*," Beck said. "I want a positive identification."

"Yes, ma'am."

Beck pulled her comlink and keyed it. "Sergeant, this is Beck. We've found the ship. Report."

There was a burst of static, then Torrent's voice came through, oddly smooth in the absence of his helmet's speakers, even over the comlink. She could hear the howl of a speeder engine and the wind.

"As you predicted, Commander. The bounty hunters headed directly to another of the berths, then proceeded from there into the city. I acquired a swoop bike to follow them. They went to a low-rent hotel on the Motok southside, near the edge of the dome, and entered the building. I remained outside behind cover, and you were right, ma'am. Wasn't more than three minutes later the two we encountered on the promenade exited with a third human, the hunters in pursuit. I wasn't able to positively ID, but I'm certain it's Ematt."

"They're being pursued?"

"Not at the moment, though two of the bounty hunters are certainly going to follow."

"Only two?"

"I had to exercise initiative to execute your plan as required, ma'am."

"Discreet, I trust?"

"Very discreet, ma'am."

"Which ones?"

"The Gran and the human had to be neutralized to allow the quarry to escape."

Beck didn't bother fighting the smile she felt, though she kept it small. "Let me know when they reach the port."

"Understood."

She paused. "Very good work, Sergeant."

"Thank you, ma'am."

Beck tucked her comlink away, then turned to the trooper with the handheld. "Anything?"

"Coming in now, Commander. Ship is identified as . . . the *Millennium Falcon*. Owner of record is a Corellian wanted on multiple counts, everything from smuggling to impersonating an Imperial officer. Name of Han Solo. Ship has a registered copilot, a Wookiee known as Chewbacca."

The trooper turned the handheld to Beck, showing her the screen where two file images of a human and a Wookiee were slowly rotating.

"The two from the promenade," Beck said. "Excellent. Corporal, I want all Imperial units on this location immediately. When they arrive, position two squads around this ship. The remaining units are to take cover outside of the bay to cut off their retreat. Make it very clear that the units outside the bay are to remain concealed until I give the order. We don't want to scare them off before they're in our trap."

The stormtrooper nodded, his helmet tilting up and down slightly, then moved off quickly to call in the other squads. Beck gazed at the ship a moment longer, then began a slow walk around it, examining it from all sides. She disliked it on principle and disliked its owner even more as a result. A ship, she felt, should reflect pride of ownership. A ship should gleam. A ship should be maintained in the best of all conditions. This ship looked as neglected as she had been in her own childhood. She felt no sympathy and no pity for what she planned to do to its owners. As for the ship itself, it would be best to impound it as Imperial salvage and melt the whole thing down.

It would be a mercy, she thought.

Her comlink trilled. "Beck."

"Five minutes out," Torrent told her. *"They're moving fast."*

"Understood. When you arrive, assume command of the units on the promenade. You'll lead them in on my signal."

"Yes, ma'am."

Beck finished her circuit around the freighter and saw that the reinforcements had arrived and were now being deployed as she had ordered. In total, she had more than forty stormtroopers in position and waiting, more than enough to deal with three enemies of the Empire. Beck took a moment to order a couple of the troopers precisely where she wanted them to wait, then took another look around the docking bay. With the stormtroopers in concealment, everything appeared as one would expect: mundane, even boring. A single door, recessed opposite the bow of the ship, led into the bay from the promenade. She paused to study the door and noted that the lights above it were glowing blue. That wouldn't do, she realized; they'd left the door into the bay unlocked, something Solo and the Wookiee were bound to notice.

"Trooper," she said. "Lock us in."

"Yes, ma'am!"

Beck took a position behind one of the landing struts to the fore of the ship, where she wouldn't be spotted when Solo, his Wookiee, and Ematt arrived. Her stomach ached gently, in anticipation and excitement. This was, she reflected, turning out to be a very good day. The trooper at the door finished working the panel, and the lights went from blue to red, indicating the lock had been thrown.

No mistakes, Beck thought. Not this time.

Three and a half minutes later, Beck's comlink called for attention again. She had it in her hand and brought it immediately to her ear.

"Beck."

"*Heading your way.*"

"Get into position. Out." She turned to address

the waiting stormtroopers, raising her chin slightly to help project her voice clearly. "All weapons are to be secured on stun. We want them alive. I repeat, we want them alive. One is a Wookiee. It will take multiple shots to put him down. No one is to fire unless I give the order."

There was the immediate muted clatter of stormtroopers in armor as each checked his E-11, making certain the blaster was set to stun.

"You are stormtroopers," she said. "You are the keenest weapon in the Emperor's arsenal. Do not fail him. Do not fail me."

From her comlink, Torrent's voice: *"On approach. Twenty seconds."*

"Your status?"

"In position."

"Wait for my order."

"Yes, ma'am."

Beck put her comlink away, drew her own blaster, and double-checked the setting, confirming she was locked on stun. This time there would be no mistakes. This time, there would be no Rodian willing to die to protect the Rebel Alliance. This time, everything was going to go as planned.

The lights over the docking bay doors switched from red to blue.

Beck raised her free hand and held it aloft. All

around the docking bay she could sense the storm-troopers tensing with anticipation, with excitement. She was feeling it herself, her heart beginning to quicken in her breast. She closed her eye and switched her cybernetic one into full spectrum just in time to watch the door snap open, to watch her quarry walk into the trap.

The one identified as Solo was leading. He was tall and surprisingly handsome, wearing boots, trousers, an off-white shirt that looked like the tunic worn beneath an Imperial officer uniform, and a black pocketed vest over top. He turned as he entered and walked backward for an instant, speaking to the two who followed him.

"She's fast," Solo was saying. "You've never been on anything faster. We'll be okay, I promise."

The second one to enter was Ematt, and the datastream from Beck's eye lit immediately with alerts as the cybernetics and the computer agreed on the identification.

WANTED FOR CRIMES AGAINST THE EMPIRE—EXTREMELY DANGEROUS—APPROACH WITH CAUTION.

All the things Beck already knew. And there he was, twenty meters away and coming closer. She fought the urge to hold her breath.

"She better be," Ematt said. "Because she looks like she needs a tow."

The Wookiee, taking up the rear, growled a response that echoed softly through the cavernous space. He was small for his species, yet still well over two meters tall, covered head to toe in a pelt that ranged from blond to chocolate brown, with touches of brass and gold, and was curly in places, straight in others. The bowcaster in his hands made him look that much more imposing.

"We're going to be fine," Solo said. "Trust me."

Beck lowered her hand, giving the signal to the troopers to move, and before she'd finished the gesture she could hear them, see them, all going into motion. They stepped out from behind the landing gear, from where they'd been concealed behind the fueling pumps, the storage crates, the loadlifters, the mammoth generators for the magnetic shield that served as the roof to the bay, keeping Cyrkon's savage atmosphere out; they slipped from the shadows at the far walls and rose up from where they'd been hiding in the scaffolding above. They moved in near-perfect unison, the sound they made terrifying and certain, and the thrill Beck felt as she came out of cover herself was as close to joy as she would ever allow herself.

The Corellian, Solo, reacted instantly with what was, to Beck, undoubtedly the quickest draw she had ever seen. His hand was empty and then it was moving, and then the blaster he wore on his thigh was free of its holster and in his hand and coming up. The Wookiee and Ematt weren't as quick, but they were fast.

None was fast enough.

Beck already had her blaster pointed at Solo.

"It's really not worth it," she said.

The Corellian looked like he was considering arguing the point. For a moment, she thought he might actually shoot her. Ematt and the Wookiee both pivoted, turning back to the exit to look for an escape. Solo started to turn with them, then stopped as Torrent—still without his armor but now with his E-11—stepped into the open doorway, the remaining stormtroopers from outside at his back. They flowed into the room like water, surrounding Solo, Ematt, and the Wookiee.

"It's over," Beck said.

Solo looked back at her. He sighed and reholstered his blaster.

"Yeah," Han Solo said. "I guess it is."

CHAPTER 10
A LITTLE HOPE

CHEWBACCA MADE A LONG, low, mournful noise, what would've sounded like a howl if there had been any volume behind it. It was the sound of despair, and frustration, and self-recrimination. It was a sound that said no good deed went unpunished.

If Solo had been a Wookiee, it's the exact sound he'd have made at that moment, too.

The stormtroopers surrounding them didn't move. He heard Chewie, behind him, make another, shorter and even gentler howl, and saw out of the corner of his eye as one of the troopers took Chewie's bowcaster. They disarmed Ematt next, then came to Solo. Reluctantly, he slid his blaster free from its holster and handed it over.

"I'm going to want that back," Solo said.

The stormtrooper didn't say anything, just stepped back. A human male, maybe in his early forties, moved up from behind them and went to the Imperial officer who had done all the talking so far. They spoke for a moment, and Solo couldn't make out what they were saying, but the man remained at her side. There was something vaguely familiar about him.

The officer strode forward, her blaster pointed pretty much directly between Solo's eyes, but she held it in such a way that it seemed somehow like an afterthought. It was the same woman from the promenade earlier, but this time Solo could get a better look at her. She was almost his height, and pretty, too, in an icy-blond sort of way that the scar didn't seem to diminish as much as that terrifying cybernetic eye did. She was brimming with arrogance and self-satisfaction; it was evident in everything she did, everything about her, from the way she moved to the way she spoke to the slight, contemptuous smile playing at her lips.

Solo thought he might just hate her on principle.

"My name is Commander Alecia Beck," she said. "You are now prisoners of the Imperial Security Bureau. You are outnumbered, outgunned, and with no hope of escape or rescue. Any resistance will be met with force. I say this to make it clear: you have no hope."

"I have a little hope," Solo said, mostly to annoy her.

It worked. The woman stepped closer.

"No," she said. "You are terrorists. You are rebels—"

"I'm not a rebel—"

"And you will meet the fate reserved for all enemies of the Empire. You will be interrogated. You will be broken. Then you will be executed."

"You'll never stop us," Ematt said, behind Solo.

Solo fought the urge to roll his eyes.

The woman shifted her gaze from Solo over his shoulder, to look at Ematt. Her smile actually grew.

"Ematt," she said. "How does it feel knowing your team sacrificed their lives, only for you to end up in my hands at the end? I should think that would hurt quite a bit."

Ematt moved forward, coming shoulder to shoulder with Solo. "You will never stop us. We will not be broken. However long it takes, we will never stop fighting."

Solo looked at Ematt. It wasn't the words, or at least not the words alone; it was how Ematt said them, the conviction of them. It was absolute, and it was fearless, and for Solo—who at that moment wasn't above feeling more than a little worried, if not outright scared—it was both surprising and admirable. He'd yet to find a cause he was willing to die for outside of his own skin, Chewbacca, and the *Falcon*. He didn't *like* the Empire, but that was mostly because he didn't like bullies, and as far as he was concerned, that's all the

Galactic Empire was: a collection of bullies who rampaged across the galaxy, pushing people around. Case in point, the Imperial officer now smirking at Ematt.

But Ematt *believed* what he was saying. He believed in what he was doing. And not just that, he believed that what he was doing was right and would prevail.

You had to admire someone with that kind of conviction, Solo thought. Either that or avoid him at all costs, and it was clearly far too late to do that.

"Never," Ematt repeated.

The Imperial officer lunged suddenly, catching Ematt by the chin and pulling him forward. At the same time, one of the stormtroopers took hold of his arms. Beck's smile vanished, and Solo took the opportunity to take a half step back, closer to Chewbacca.

"You will tell us everything," Beck said. "By the time I am finished with you, you will be *begging* to tell me everything, Ematt."

She released him, and the stormtrooper pulled Ematt upright again. Beck turned to the man standing beside her. "Binders on all of them. Search them. I want a transport immediately to move them aboard *Vehement*."

"Yes, ma'am."

Chewie tilted his head, and Solo felt hair brushing his ear as the Wookiee rumbled quietly.

"I'm working on it," Solo said.

"Quiet," one of the stormtroopers said.

"Sure, sure." Solo looked around, trying to be subtle about it. There had to be a way out, but he wasn't seeing it. With forty or more stormtroopers surrounding the three of them, much as he hated to admit it, they were out of moves. If he could get aboard the *Falcon* there were options. The ship was plated with military-grade armor that would easily shrug off the small-arms fire from the blaster rifles and keep them safe. There were a couple of other surprises packed aboard, too. But it meant getting to the ship, and he could already tell that Beck wasn't about to let that happen. There was no way to get aboard without getting shot to pieces in the process.

What else? The bay was littered with exactly the sorts of things he'd come to expect from such places. Crates of replacement parts scattered here and there, the refueling system, its pressure pumps and hoses— that could be a big boom if he could somehow disrupt it—the great big magnetic-field generators maintaining the energy barrier overhead. Solo glanced up, saw the shimmering blue, Cyrkon's polluted night sky above glowing a dull reddish brown, *Miss Fortune* coming slowly into view, riding its repulsors silently, the distant air traffic gliding past beyond, the—

Solo blinked and nudged Chewie with his elbow, using his eyes to direct the Wookiee's gaze skyward.

Miss Fortune was making a slow turn, almost hovering now. As they watched, the ventral hatch on the yacht slid open, and a moment later the turret dropped into place, rotating to point at them.

She's out of her mind, Solo thought.

The stormtrooper without armor—because that's what he was, Solo had decided—was searching Ematt, and being thorough about it. Another trooper stood with him, holding three sets of binders.

Chewie huffed.

"The magnetic shield is still up," Solo said.

Chewie huffed again. There was a look in his blue eyes.

"It's not my fault." Solo turned suddenly, stepping closer to the Wookiee until their chests were almost butting. "And I don't want to hear talk like that again."

"I told you to be quiet—" the stormtrooper said.

"You tell *him* to be quiet," Solo snapped.

Beck glared at them both, and Ematt twisted where he stood, his hands now out in front of him, the binders ready to snap onto his wrists.

Chewie leaned down and growled loudly, blasting Solo with hot breath and calling him something that Solo would've been ashamed to say to his own mother.

"Listen, furball," Solo said. "You say that again I'll make you regret it."

"Get your Wookiee under control," Beck said.

Chewie snarled, showing Solo his teeth. He said it again.

"That's it. I've had enough out of you," Solo said, and he swung and punched Chewie in the jaw. It was a good punch, and on anyone else it would've certainly rocked him, if not knocked him back on the seat of his pants.

Chewie barely moved his head. He roared and both hands came up. Then with all of his substantial Wookiee strength, he shoved Solo, sending him flying back into the stormtrooper behind him. The first collision caused a second, then a third, a clatter of armor hitting the floor and Solo landing atop the pile. Stormtroopers were pointing their rifles at Chewie, but the Wookiee lashed out, catching one alongside his helmet and sending him tumbling. He grabbed another one and literally swung him at yet a third.

"Stun him!" Beck shouted.

Solo, still atop the stormtrooper Chewbacca had thrown him into, twisted and wrenched the blaster rifle from the trooper's hand. He thumbed the selector to turn the weapon from stun, raising it and rolling all at once. He put the sights on the generator nearest him and fired. Blaster bolts flew and smashed into the machinery, bursting through its exterior casing, and Solo fired again. The generator blew, exploding into fragments and fire, and then Solo was up on a knee and sighting at the second generator, across the bay. He knew it was a much harder shot, but he fired anyway. The second generator blew at once, and above them the magnetic shield vanished, immediately replaced by the howling of the heated, toxic air rushing into the docking bay. Tiny particles of smog stung his eyes and instantly coated the back of his throat. Solo felt himself immediately beginning to perspire, and just as immediately felt the sweat evaporating from his skin.

Everyone was moving at once, now, Chewie roaring. Beck was wheeling around in place, her blaster coming up, and Ematt and the stormtrooper without armor were grappling with each other.

"Get down!" Solo shouted and launched himself at Ematt, catching the man around the waist and dragging him to the deck just as *Miss Fortune* opened fire from its belly turret.

The first salvo of shots slammed straight into the group of stormtroopers Solo had left behind. He heard shouts, cries of pain, and scrambled to his feet, dragging Ematt with him. Chewie was already halfway to the *Falcon*, dropping the ramp, and Solo all but threw Ematt after him. His eyes and throat were burning from the pollution, the foul atmosphere already feeling like it was corroding his flesh. The heat was climbing; it had its own weight, trying to cook him inside and out. The stormtrooper who had taken their weapons was flat on the ground, facedown, hit by the turret fire.

"Run! Go!"

Another salvo from above, too close for Solo's comfort as he dropped the E-11 and scooped up his and Chewie's weapons. Stormtroopers were firing, but *Miss Fortune*'s salvos were forcing them into cover, and now Solo was racing after Ematt, who was sprinting for the ramp. Chewie was out of sight, already inside. Solo saw Beck screaming orders, saw her raising her blaster, and then the stormtrooper without armor was pulling her into cover. An instant later *Miss Fortune* was racking shots where the Imperial officer had been standing. Solo was almost at the ship when he felt his right leg go suddenly numb as he was grazed by a stun bolt. He managed to collapse on the ramp as it began to raise. Ematt pulled him forward, into the safety of the *Falcon*.

"Chewie! Time to leave!" Solo pulled himself upright using Ematt and the side of the hull, then half hopped, half limped through the main compartment and toward the cockpit. The ship came to life beneath his boots; he could feel it leaping suddenly into the air. Sweat ran into his eyes, making them sting. Ematt stumbled and Solo had to brace himself, and then he was in the cockpit and falling into the pilot's seat.

"Told you I'd think of something," he said, reaching for the headset with one hand and taking the yoke with the other.

Chewie barked and slapped a battery of switches. Behind them, Ematt was taking the navigator's seat and already strapping himself in.

"You two play it fast and loose," Ematt said.

"It's worked so far."

Chewie snorted.

"I barely touched you." Solo finished setting the comlink headset in place and turned on the speakers in the cockpit. "I'm the one who's gonna be bruised, pal. *Miss Fortune*, this is the *Falcon*."

"Figured I owed you one, Han."

"This settles my tab?"

"Not on your life," Delia said. *"You get him?"*

"I'm here, Delia," Ematt said. "Nice friends you've got."

"Beggars can't be choosers. I'm thinking it's time for all of us to get out of here."

Chewie rumbled in agreement, and Solo rocked the throttle forward, bringing the *Falcon* off of repulsors and feathering the engines to life. The ship responded, surging and eager, and already outside the canopy Solo could see the pollution of Cyrkon melting away, the stars springing into view. Off the starboard side, the *Miss Fortune* was keeping pace, wisps of the upper atmosphere streaming from the ship's hull like smoke from a dying fire.

The *Falcon* began bleating, and Chewie checked his

deck, slapped another two switches, and reached up behind him, powering up the weapons. Solo glanced at his sensors and twisted to stab one of the buttons on the navicomputer, bringing it to life.

"Angle the deflectors," he said to Chewie, then pointed at Ematt. "You better know where we're going."

"I know where we're going."

"Feed it to the navicomputer." Solo twisted back. His leg was beginning to throb, the stun wearing off. Ahead of them and far too big, the Star Destroyer was turning into view, a flight of tiny dots in tight formation heading their direction from beneath the massive vessel. "Delia, eight marks at one-one."

"We see them. TIEs."

"How long until you can make the jump to lightspeed?"

"Couple of minutes."

"Just stay away from that Star Destroyer."

"You think?"

"Destination is programmed," Ematt said as the navicomputer beeped. "It'll take a couple minutes before the jump is plotted. Can we hold them off?"

Solo checked his sensors again, then the view from the cockpit. The TIEs were closing in, fast.

"I don't think we have a choice," he said.

CHAPTER 11
VEHEMENT'S GRIP

BECK COULD TASTE blood in her mouth, where she'd bitten her own lip when Torrent had saved her life. She had no doubt that was what he had done, either; while she'd understood the Corellian and the Wookiee were playing at something, the attack from above had been entirely unexpected. She just had never accounted for the possibility that the rebels might have close air support, and it was a mistake that had cost her—the same way the Rodian's willingness to die had cost her, the same way she had never imagined it was an act of which any rebel was capable. Another miscalculation on her part, one she would never make again.

Half her stormtroopers were dead or wounded, hit by blasts from the ship overhead. She could easily have been among them. Her normal eye stung, tears running down her cheek from the sickening air that now howled through the docking bay, but the tears evaporated almost as quickly as they appeared, leaving salt stuck to her cheek. The heat was ghastly and turned her mouth dry. She winked, trying to clear her good eye, speaking to the comlink in her hand.

"*Vehement*, respond."

"*Captain Hove.*"

"Two ships just took off, the YT-1300 and another. I want those ships, Captain. I want those ships, I want the crews, I want them alive."

"*They just appeared on our scopes.*"

"They do not make hyperspace, is that clear?"

"*We're not an Interdictor, Commander. We don't have the ability to—*"

"No excuses!" Beck was shouting, she realized. Rising over the wind came the roar of the transport as it slid into place overhead and began to come in for a landing. "I'm on my way up. Do *not* allow those ships to escape!"

"*As you order, Commander.*"

The transport was down, its main ramp dropping.

"With me," Beck said.

Torrent rose from where he'd been kneeling by one of the dead stormtroopers. His expression was grim, and she wondered if the trooper had been a friend, wondered how Torrent could tell the troopers apart when they were all in identical armor. He got to his feet.

"Let's move," he told the remaining stormtroopers.

Quickly and as a unit they filed into the back of the transport. Beck hit the panel to raise the ramp, and the ship was lifting off before the pressure seals had locked, the foul atmosphere of Cyrkon abruptly banished. Beck coughed, clearing her lungs, and felt as if something was trying to scrape open her throat. The stormtroopers, in their helmets, had been spared the worst of the noxious air. Torrent hacked a couple of times. Beck wiped the tears still streaming down her unmarred cheek and made her way to the cockpit.

"I want to be on the *Vehement* in three minutes," she told the pilot.

The pilot nodded and gave the ship full throttle. The engines rose to a fever pitch, the atmosphere burned past, and ahead of her Beck could see the Star Destroyer, enormous and imposing and appearing much closer than it was. The two smaller ships, the *Millennium Falcon* and the other, unidentified vessel, appeared minuscule in comparison, even as the transport banked to give them wide berth.

"*Miss Fortune*," Torrent said from over her shoulder. She glanced back and saw that he was looking past her at the same view. "It's the ship I tracked the bounty hunters to before following them into Motok."

Beck nodded slightly, making a mental note to further investigate *Miss Fortune*. There was no way to engage either ship, not in the transport. They had to avoid them, had to get back to the *Vehement* where she would be able to assert some control over the situation once more. Knowing all this didn't help her, didn't relieve the feeling of powerlessness consuming her, the growing frustration.

"They'll need a few minutes before they can jump to hyperspace," Beck said. "We can still catch them."

"Yes, ma'am," Torrent said.

For the first time, she thought he sounded less than enthusiastic.

The second flight of TIEs screamed past them as the transport made its final approach. Beck waited impatiently as the ship completed its landing in the main ventral bay of the *Vehement*, and as soon as she felt the ship locking down, she was hitting the release and exiting before the ramp had completely lowered. She ran, not caring who saw, to the main lift, shoved aside the two lieutenants waiting for the car to arrive, stepped in, and headed for the bridge.

She emerged into a calm that immediately annoyed her. Captain Hove stood with his back to her at the far end of the Star Destroyer's bridge, staring out the viewport, his hands clasped behind him. She ran down the central walkway, the command and control pits on either side, slowed to a jog, then a walk. Hove heard her coming and turned to greet her.

"Commander Beck. Two flights launched and engaged, we—"

"Move us in closer. I want tractor beams on those two ships, the *Falcon* and the other one."

Hove closed his mouth tightly and arched an eyebrow. "There are eight TIE fighters—"

"Yes, I heard you, Captain. I'm wondering if you heard me."

He looked distinctly uncomfortable and glanced to his right, looking past Beck to the array of crew and officers all doing their best to appear not to be listening. Beck didn't care if they were overheard, but Hove obviously did, and he lowered his voice, stepping closer.

"Commander, the TIEs are engaged with the enemy. Activating the tractor beam risks capturing our ships, as well as the quarry."

"I am aware."

"The modulation required to capture the quarry will tear a TIE apart if it also finds itself caught in the tractor beam."

"I am aware of that, as well." Beck fixed him with a stare. "Is this a problem, Captain?"

Hove spoke slowly. "Those are our pilots, Commander."

"You insist on stating the obvious, Captain. You have my orders. Execute them at once, or I shall have you arrested for dereliction of duty and aiding and abetting the enemy."

Hove's jaw tightened, his back straightened. He inclined his head, clicked his heels, then turned to face the command deck.

"Close to tractor beam range," he ordered, and Beck was somewhat mollified to find no hesitation or uncertainty in his voice as he spoke. "Target the freighter and the yacht."

The order was echoed around the bridge, a flurry of motion at the helm. The Star Destroyer began its turn to port, and through the bridge windows Beck could see *Miss Fortune* and the *Millennium Falcon* once more, still small but gradually coming closer. Flashes of turbolaser fire cut the darkness, needles of red and green and blue slicing through space as the ten ships twisted and spun and danced together in combat.

"Beam control, confirm," Hove said.

The response was immediate, loud and clear. "At your order, Captain."

"Time to target?"

"One minute, eleven seconds."

Hove turned to face the windows again and canted his head slightly toward Beck. "It will be close, but we should catch them before they can make the jump to hyperspace."

Beck kept her eyes on the battle, slowly coming closer. One of the TIEs tried to cut across the *Falcon*'s stern, sweeping into another pass, and a line of green reached out from *Miss Fortune* and touched the fighter along one solar panel. The TIE broke apart, exploding an instant later. Seven against two.

"For your sake, Captain," Beck said, "I hope you're correct."

CHAPTER 12
TRYING TO BE NOBLE

"**G**OT THREE MORE coming around, starboard at two-eight mark seven!" Ematt said.
Chewie snarled.

"What'd he say?"

"He said, 'Shoot them.'" Solo played the throttle, dropping thrust on the *Falcon*'s starboard sublight engine and at the same time pulling the yoke to the left and back, bringing the ship around in a nearly uncontrolled spin and loop. The artificial gravity aboard the *Falcon*, a fraction of a second behind the maneuver, struggled to compensate, and Solo nearly flew free of the pilot's seat. Chewbacca snorted.

"I'll strap in when I'm not trying to keep us all from dying," Solo retorted. "Delia, how you doing?"

"We've had better days!"

Another TIE seemed to come out of nowhere, firing

as it went, and shot overhead so close Solo was certain he could see the pilot in the fighter's tiny cockpit. The *Falcon* shuddered as laser fire raked the dorsal hull. The deflector display to Chewbacca's left flashed, the small graphic representation of the ship that had been glowing green to indicate the shields were at full power now beginning to shift to yellow. The Wookiee reached under the console, pulled a coil of wiring free with an attendant burst of sparks, and shoved the end into one of the sockets at his right elbow. The display flared, the yellow vanished, and the green returned.

"That'll work for now," Solo said. "Hold on."

Outside the canopy, the starfield whirled like someone was trying to send it down a drain as Solo brought the starboard engine back to match thrust with the other two propelling the *Falcon*. They shot forward, the ship now rapidly rolling around and around as it went.

"I can't get a shot if you do that!" Ematt said.

"I'm giving you a shot," Solo said. "Get ready."

The *Falcon* came out of its last roll and Solo jinked to port, then dipped the nose before yanking back on the yoke, hard, putting the ship into a tight Corellian turn and inverting their flight and direction. The TIEs that had fallen off with the *Falcon*'s acceleration reappeared dead ahead, closing fast, four of them in tight attack formation. Chewie chortled.

"Money lane shot," Solo said. "Do it!"

Ematt worked the *Falcon*'s turbolasers, the two turrets mounted atop and beneath the ship. Normally—ideally—Solo would man one of the guns and either Chewie or another warm body the other, but their current situation clearly didn't allow for that. Solo and Chewie were both required in the cockpit. It wasn't the first time Solo had found himself in this situation, and he and Chewbacca had accounted for it by running auxiliary fire control through the cockpit. It wasn't as accurate as manning the guns individually, and it relied heavily on computer assist, but if Ematt knew what he was doing, he'd be able to down at least one of the TIEs. Solo had handed him the shot on a plate.

Ematt knew what he was doing. A flare of light burst off to Solo's left as the dorsal turbolasers fired, and one of the approaching TIEs bloomed into a cascade of fire and debris. The remaining fighters tried to split, two to port, one to starboard; Ematt opened up with the ventral turret, and a second TIE exploded into nothingness, vaporized by a direct hit.

"Okay," Solo said. "That wasn't bad."

"Han! One-four mark six!"

Solo put the *Falcon* into another roll, this time swooping around to eyeball the coordinates Delia had given. The *Vehement* was looming closer, much closer than it had been before.

"They're moving to tractor beam range," Solo said.

One of the computers at the navigation station chirped, then chortled.

"We've got the jump," Ematt said. "Let's get out of here!"

"Delia, we're good to go." Solo banked, the two remaining TIEs still pursuing them and skimming past to port, firing as they came. The *Falcon* rocked again, the shield display flashing, the green disappearing into a wash of yellow. They were losing their shields.

Miss Fortune came into view through the cockpit, the little yacht looping in an attempt to shake the three TIE fighters still relentlessly attacking. As he watched, one of the TIEs fired a salvo that raked along *Miss Fortune*'s hull, shots flashing and dissipating along its shields. There was a flare of light, then a burst of debris from atop the yacht.

"Delia—"

There was static over the comms, harsh white noise for an instant, then Delia Leighton's voice, threaded with barely restrained panic.

"We just lost our navicomputer! We don't have a jump!"

"You still have auxiliary?"

Curtis's voice came over the speakers for the first time. *"It's gonna be another minute before we can run the bypass."*

"We take another hit like that, we're dead in space!" The edges of panic in Delia's voice were clearer.

Chewbacca barked and looked at Solo.

It wasn't good. A quick check of the sensors showed that the Star Destroyer would be in tractor beam range inside twenty seconds. They had their coordinates plotted, and the hyperdrive was ready; all it would take was a turn to the proper heading and kicking into lightspeed and Solo, Chewbacca, Ematt, the *Falcon*, all of them would be instantly and safely away from the Empire's grip. They could leave right now—mission accomplished.

But it would leave *Miss Fortune* behind, exposed, vulnerable. It would mean that Delia and Curtis would be captured, brought aboard *Vehement*. They would be interrogated and tortured. At best, the crew of *Miss Fortune* would spend the rest of their lives on some Imperial penal world.

At worst, they'd never leave the *Vehement* alive.

Chewie was still looking at Solo. He could feel Ematt behind him, doing the same.

"You better clear my tab at the bar after this," Solo muttered.

He pushed the throttles forward, feeling the *Falcon* surge, and slapped the illegal SLAM activator he'd installed to give the ship an additional burst of speed.

Miss Fortune zoomed closer, the TIEs on its tail still swirling around it like angry insects eager to feast. Ematt opened fire and clipped one of the TIEs, sending it twirling away toward the nimbus glow of Cyrkon's atmosphere, fired again and caught another with a graze along the cockpit ball. Atmosphere immediately erupted from the perforated cabin in a cloud of white and gray vapor as the TIE splintered into jagged pieces of metal.

"*Han, go.*" Delia suddenly sounded much calmer. "*That Star Destroyer's unbeatable. We're done here. We're not going to have the jump in time.*"

The *Falcon* jolted, shields fading from yellow to red. Three TIE fighters and a Star Destroyer. Delia was correct—there was no way to win that particular fight.

"We're covering you," Solo said.

"*Han—*"

"Delia, shut up. I'm trying to be noble."

He heard her laugh over the speakers.

Aboard *Vehement*, Beck watched as the number of TIE fighters steadily diminished, what had been eight now reduced to three. Something was wrong with the yacht, though; she'd seen it take a hit, seen the debris fly. The *Falcon* was another matter. TIEs had scored direct hits on its aft section above the engines, twice along the dorsal line, and once near the mandibles that jutted at the front of the freighter, but not one of the shots had seemed to have any appreciable effect.

It didn't matter. They were in range.

"Captain Hove."

Hove half turned and gestured with his right hand toward the pit. "At maximum power," he ordered.

"Target locked," came the reply. "Tractor beam at maximum power."

There was no visible response from the emitters at the fore of the Star Destroyer. Unlike turbolasers, the energy field for the tractor beam was outside the visible spectrum, but through her cybernetic eye Beck could see it. She could see it all: the conelike ray slowly flowing away from them, a semitransparent wave of gold that spread inexorably toward the five ships.

It first struck one of the TIEs pursuing the *Falcon* and yanked it back as if on a leash, taking the fighter's velocity and suddenly, even cruelly, stealing it away. The stress was too much for the little fighter; the twin solar panels on either side tore apart like it was a child's toy broken in an angry tantrum. The ball of the cockpit hung motionless, suspended, then crushed in on itself.

Beside Beck, Hove turned away.

The beam continued its advance.

"No escape," Beck said.

————

"They catch us in that tractor beam, we're done," Ematt said. "I can't let them take me alive, you understand that?"

"They're not taking any of us," Solo said with far more conviction than he was feeling.

Chewie whuffed, quickly rebalancing power from the engines to the shields again. For the second time, he pulled the cord of wiring and plugged it into yet another socket.

"I'm working on it," Han replied. He clicked on the comms again. "Delia, you and Curtis make a run for the atmosphere and we'll cover you. How long until you've got your jump?"

"Another fifteen seconds," Curtis said.

Miss Fortune broke suddenly to its starboard, banking tightly, and Solo twisted the *Falcon* around to follow, closing the distance between it and the TIE fighter between them. The last of the TIEs pursuing them, behind the *Falcon*, pulled up abruptly, and on the rear monitor Solo watched as it met the fate of its partner, the tractor beam from the Star Destroyer tearing it to shreds. He felt something sickening and hard forming in his stomach; he had no love for the Empire, but the willing sacrifice of their own pilots, their own ships, in pursuit of the *Falcon* and *Miss Fortune* was a level of brutality beyond what he had ever seen. Whoever was giving orders on *Vehement* would stop at nothing to catch them.

A mournful, soft woof came from Chewie. Solo didn't bother saying anything. He and the Wookiee were thinking the same thing.

Miss Fortune was accelerating, now pulled tighter by Cyrkon's gravity, the remaining TIE still gamely following and the *Falcon* closing in behind. Solo heard Ematt lining up his shot and brought the yoke up just a fraction to allow both turrets a clear field of fire. The targeting computer beeped slowly, then more and more rapidly as the TIE came into range, then trilled loudly, signifying a lock. The *Falcon* vibrated slightly as both turrets fired together, turbolaser bolts converging on the fighter, tracking onto the center ball. The fighter burst like a punctured balloon, shards of metal spraying in all directions.

"Shut down the weapons," Solo said over his shoulder. "Chewie, reroute all power to the engines, stand by to cut off on my order."

"Full power won't be enough to get away from that tractor beam," Ematt said.

"I know what I'm doing."

The *Falcon* jerked, engines suddenly shrieking in protest as the whole ship shuddered, slowing rapidly.

"Cut them," Solo said.

Chewbacca moved without hesitation, long arms rising to strike the rows of engine cutoff switches overhead. The *Falcon* went suddenly silent, its engines guttering out. They were still moving forward, momentum and Cyrkon's gravity each working on the ship, but they were slowing, and slowing quickly. It was going to be very close.

"Delia?"

"Five seconds."

Solo eyed the sensors again and nudged the yoke, adjusting the *Falcon's* approach to the planet. They were in the outer atmosphere; he could see the faint shimmer beginning to surround the cockpit.

"I hope you know what you're doing," Ematt said.

"I always know what I'm doing," Solo lied.

"What are they doing?" Beck demanded.

"I'm not certain, Commander." Hove checked over his shoulder. "We have the ship?"

"We're having trouble establishing the lock," the officer at the tractor beam control said. The reluctance in his voice was unmistakable. "Interference from the planet's gravity. The beam keeps slipping."

"Then bring us in closer," Beck said.

Hove hesitated, then nodded. The second ship, *Miss Fortune*, was still out of range, but Beck could live with that. Ematt was aboard the *Millennium Falcon*, and that was the ship she wanted. That was the ship she was going to take. *Miss Fortune* and her crew could be tracked down and punished later, but their capture was, at this moment, incidental. The prize was the *Millennium Falcon*. The prize was that ship, and its crew.

The Star Destroyer continued its pursuit, Cyrkon now filling the view, a haze of polluted atmosphere. *Miss Fortune* was pulling up, using the planet's gravity to help slingshot back into space, but the *Falcon* was now on what appeared to be a dive, as if its captain intended to bury the ship in the planet's surface. The stress on the hull of the little freighter must have been enormous, certainly more than it should be able to endure, from the looks of it; yet it was holding together. And while it was coming closer, it was not, Beck felt, doing so nearly quickly enough.

"Where are they heading?" Hove asked.

Caught between free fall and the slackening grip of the *Vehement*'s tractor beam, the *Millennium Falcon* trembled and hopped, the atmosphere around the ship growing thicker and thicker. The distant, faint outline of the domed capital began to resolve below. Solo nudged the yoke and risked using the landing jets, separate from the now-cooling engines, to adjust the ship's angle.

"Delia . . ."

"Coming up. . . . We've got it, we're ready!"

"Then what are you waiting for? Go!"

"Han . . ."

"Delia, you're still talking! Go!"

"The next one's on the house," Delia Leighton said.

The comms went dead—no static, just the heavy presence of empty air. Chewie chuffed and adjusted his grip on his own yoke. On the sensors, Miss Fortune vanished, launched into hyperspace.

There was silence in the cockpit for several seconds.

"So, your plan is to crash into Motok?" Ematt asked. It sounded very conversational.

"Ideally, no," Solo said.

"Telemetry puts them on approach to the capital," someone answered.

"Pull them back," Beck said.

"We're trying, Commander," the beam officer said. He looked up at her from the command pit, helpless. "Our lock won't maintain. This is the best we can do at this range."

"Then bring us *closer*!"

"You want us to follow them into the atmosphere?" Hove asked.

"If that's what it takes."

"Commander, if we attempt to tractor beam them within the atmosphere, without a precise lock . . . the beam will splash. There will be overlap. Collateral damage to the planet could be immense."

"If that's what it takes," Beck repeated.

"We'll destroy the dome," Hove said. "We'll shred the protection around Motok, Commander. We'll destroy the city."

Beck saw it, then, saw what Han Solo and the Wookiee were doing with their ship, the gamble they had made. Yes, *Vehement* could follow them down, could stop them, could pull them back with its tractor beam. But in so doing, it would render Motok inhospitable. It would decimate the city, and do it before millions and millions of witnesses on the ground who would see the Star Destroyer overhead and not see the tiny YT-1300 stock freighter they were pursuing. Those who didn't die from exposure to the planet's toxic atmosphere would know only that the Empire had destroyed their home. They would remember. They would share. Even with the Empire's control over the media, the word would spread and people would hear. Some of those people would demand an explanation, and more would demand vengeance. And among those, some would take action.

Some would become rebels.

Hove was waiting for her order. The entirety of the bridge, the whole of *Vehement* was waiting for her order. She thought about the freighter, the *Millennium Falcon*, and its crew—three people against the might of the Empire. A ship that looked as though it could barely fly, that had shrugged off TIE fighters, that had maneuvered itself into a dead-engine glide, that was daring her—daring *her*—to catch it, at the price of turning an entire world against the Galactic Empire.

Without a word, she turned on her toe and began the long walk past the command and control pits, to the elevator.

The failure, she knew, was hers and hers alone.

The *Falcon* shuddered, and suddenly they weren't gliding as much as plummeting, Motok rising rapidly before them.

"Engines, Chewie!" Solo yanked the yoke with one hand and brought both feet down hard on the pedals for the landing jets. His free hand flailed, caught the master switch for the repulsorlift generators, and threw them to life. The ship groaned, creaking as multiple stresses played all at once across its hull.

"We're still falling," Ematt observed.

"Chewie, the engines!"

The Wookiee howled, then smashed a fist into the console. A grinding noise rose from the back of the ship, then faded, then rose, then faded again, this time with a pathetic cough.

"Still falling."

"I know!" Motok was coming closer. Very quickly. "Open the manifold on the primary thrust!"

The Wookiee punched the console again, this time leaving a visible dent, then reached past Solo and twisted one of the larger handles fixed to the wall. The engines gasped, the grinding noise returning.

"Still—"

"Say it again and you're getting out and walking." Solo lunged out of his seat, almost splaying himself across Chewbacca as the Wookiee did something similar in the opposite direction. "On three, Chewie, manual restart. One . . . two . . . three—"

Each of them yanked on separate levers simultaneously. The engines coughed, protested, and suddenly roared. Pilot and copilot scrambled upright, took hold of their respective yokes, and pulled. Motok, frighteningly close below and growing closer, seemed to spread out before them as the *Falcon*'s nose came up, and Solo could swear the belly of the ship kissed the top of the dome as they leveled off, then began to climb. He pushed the throttles forward, felt the *Falcon*'s engines singing to him, and they were looking at stars again, the Star Destroyer now well out of tractor beam range on their sensors. The proximity alarm warned of more TIE fighters being launched, twelve of them this time, but it didn't matter.

Solo grinned, reaching with one hand for the hyperspace engage. With his other, he stroked the side of the console nearest him.

"Don't ever scare me like that again, baby," Han Solo said, and he gently pushed the lever forward.

The *Falcon*'s response was to leap them into hyperspace—and to safety.

EPILOGUE

"AND . . . ?" THE WOMAN SAID.

The old man tilted his head, glanced past the three around the table who'd listened to his tale, and then settled his gaze on the woman once more. He rubbed the scar on his chin with an index finger.

"And what?" he said. "They got away. Ematt made it to the rendezvous and the Rebellion continued to grow. You heard of the Battle of Hoth, right? This was a few years before that. There was still a long way to go before Endor and everything that came after."

"That is the biggest load of poodoo I have *ever* heard," Strater said. His frustration brought color to his head and made the Twi'lek woman tattooed along his scalp look as if she'd suddenly had too much sun.

The old man shrugged. "Thing about the galaxy, there's as many versions of the truth as there are stars. Got an old friend who's fond of saying that truth is greatly dependent on your point of view. Truth ain't the same as fact, kid. You believe what you want to believe."

"I've never even *heard* of Cyrkon." The woman folded her arms, looking annoyed.

The old man shrugged again. His glass was empty, and he slid it away from himself across the tabletop. When he brought his eyes back up, he found the burly one staring at him. He was their leader, the old man had determined, and he hadn't spoken once throughout the entirety of the tale. About the time the old man had begun describing the escape from Motok, the burly one's attention had seemed to wander, moving to the bar, the patrons, the bartender, even the bouncer. His hands had been out of sight since then, below the level of the table. But now the old man had his attention again.

"That's a very conveniently told story," the burly one said. "That's a story full of some very nice coincidences."

"Hey, yeah," Strater said. "Like how you're talking about a bar that's in a ship in a port and we're in a bar in a ship in a port."

The woman looked toward the entrance of the cargo

bay and stared at the bouncer for a moment. "With a Shistavanen bouncer working the door."

"And a redhead at the bar."

The old man said nothing. He'd had one hand beneath the table himself for the past half hour, and now his fingers began to wrap around the grip of the heavy blaster holstered on his thigh.

"They could've changed the name," Strater said.

"You idiot." The burly one didn't look away from the old man, but he was clearly responding to his tattooed friend. "Of course they changed the name. *Serendipity*. He even said that was what the name meant in the original Durese."

The old man met the burly one's stare, then glanced over the man's shoulder again. He grinned. "So who're you with? The Irving Boys? Or the Guavians? Or Ducain? I'd put money on Ducain. He always went low rent on the hired help."

There was a moment's pause before the credit dropped. The burly one moved first, his hands reappearing above the table, a blaster in each. The woman, a half fraction behind him, yanked the haft of her vibro-axe from where it rode on her back and thumbed the activator as she brought it close to the old man's throat. The weapon hummed, and the old man could feel the rapid cycle of the blade's near-invisible vibration through the air, in his teeth. Strater was the slowest, the last to figure it out, fumbling his own weapon up and flushing even darker with the embarrassment of having been played for a fool.

"Solo," the burly one said.

"You want to be careful with that?" Han Solo used his free hand to push the vibro-axe's handle gently, trying to move the blade away from his throat. "Guy could get hurt."

Neither the axe nor the woman budged.

"Seriously," Solo said.

The burly one set both elbows on the table, each of his blasters now pointing directly at Solo's face. He spoke conversationally, relaxed, clearly certain the situation was his to control.

"We want the ship," the burly one said. "That's it. You hand over the *Falcon* and maybe you walk away."

Solo smiled, then found himself grinning in a way he hadn't in years. "That sounds like an unfair deal, actually."

"It's the best you're going to get, old man."

Solo considered the distance between the vibro-axe and his throat and decided it was far enough to risk shaking his head. "I don't think so. I think I've got a counter offer."

"You've got nothing to bargain with."

From behind him, at the bar, Delia Leighton said, "He's got this."

Solo didn't turn to see what she was doing, but he didn't need to. The *Miss Fortune* may have changed its name once or twice, or even half a dozen times in the past thirty-odd years—he'd honestly lost count. And it may have seen a few modifications here and there— a new waitress to replace the busted droid, another coat of paint—but some things had stayed the same. The drinks were still overpriced but poured fair and strong. Curtis still worked the door, as much as the entrance to the cargo bay could be called a door.

And Delia Leighton still worked the bar with her Scattermaster close at hand.

"You fire that thing, you'll hit him, too," the woman said.

"That's all right," Delia said. "He still hasn't settled his tab, so I'll call it even."

"Hey," Solo said. "I'm good for it."

The burly one gritted his teeth. "You're bluffing."

"Three of us, two of you," Strater said.

"You want to count again," Solo said.

"You think we've forgotten about the bouncer? He's not gonna reach you in time."

Solo shook his head again, felt the distortion from the axe tickling his beard.

"Thing people forget about Wookiees," Solo said. "They remember that they're very strong. They remember they've got a temper. They remember, maybe, that they're from Kashyyyk. But they forget one thing."

The burly one glanced at his companions, just an edge of nervousness now evident. He readjusted his grip on his weapons.

"What's that?" he asked.

"They can be very, very quiet when it suits them," Solo said. "Isn't that right, Chewie?"

The Wookiee, who had been standing behind the burly man's chair for the past dozen seconds, growled. In one swift motion, Chewie took hold of the man by the shoulders, hoisted him smoothly from his chair, and sent him flying roughly in the direction of Curtis and the door. Solo took that opportunity to grab the shaft of the vibro-axe with his free hand, forcing it away from his neck, and pointed his blaster at the woman's face with the other. Strater started up, trying to rise, but Chewbacca simply reached out and planted one big hand on his tattooed head, slamming him back down again.

Solo pulled the vibro-axe free of the woman's grasp, tossed it aside, then reached out and took the blaster from her shoulder holster and sent it sailing in the same direction. Chewie had already disarmed Strater. Solo slid his chair back and got to his feet.

"You tell Ducain, you tell the Irving Boys, you tell all of them this: we're not afraid of them," Solo said.

The woman glared up at him.

"Yeah," Solo said. "You've got a little Commander Beck to you, you know that?"

Chewie rumbled softly.

Solo half turned to Delia. "Thanks for the drinks, Captain."

"You still haven't settled your tab."

Chewbacca chuckled. Solo looked wounded. "I said I'm good for it."

"I've been hearing that a long time."

The smuggler holstered his blaster and looked around the bar. The burly one was out cold, Curtis already hauling him through the doors. Strater and the woman were glowering at him, but they weren't going to move, not now.

"Next time, Delia. I promise."

"Holding you to that."

"C'mon, Chewie."

They started for the exit, side by side, the Wookiee towering over the Corellian. They came down the ramp as Curtis was dusting his paws, the burly man propped against the near wall of the docking bay, disarmed and still unconscious.

"Hey," Curtis said. "Whatever happened with Beck?"

Chewbacca chuffed and barked.

"Tell you next time," Solo said.